Friendship a

By Alison J.

ISBN: 978-1-326-88702-5

PublishNation
www.publishnation.co.uk

To Emma and Owen

"Don't cry because it's over. Smile because it happened" Dr Seuss

Prologue

North London 2015

As Emma walked into the classroom, the feeling of dread crept slowly over her like a familiar old cardigan. It was nearly the end of break, the room was empty, a slant of sunlight, dust dancing, the debris of lesson two still strewn about the place, screwed up bits of paper on the floor just shy of the bin; the odd broken pencil; a drinking straw from a surreptitious squashed carton of juice lying nearby; a textbook with its spine bent back (a closer look will reveal rude graffiti all over the font cover). The fusty smell of fellow teenager's body odour crept into her nostrils. It was only the third week into the new school year, the end of September already. And already she hated it.

Emma placed her things neatly onto her desk, and sat down to wait. The class would arrive any minute, trailing their own brand of destruction. A moment of calm. This time it would be different. This time the teacher, Miss Ryan, would take control. There wouldn't be time for any sneery comments or "evil" looks. The class would be so engaged in the History lesson that Miss Ryan had planned for them, they wouldn't have time to draw breath, let alone draw rude things in text books! Yes, this time, Emma would not be afraid, this time she would not be bullied.

As soon as the door burst open, Emma knew that she was wrong. Miss Ryan swooped in with the rabble of the class behind her. "Come in and sit down quietly" Her voice, drowned out with the chatter; the scraping of chairs. "Hurry up now" she called, her voice already strained, threatening to break. The chatter rose in volume as they took their seats. Turning round, twisting to continue the conversations started in the playground. Not bothering to take out

1

their books; their pencil cases; the all- important homework diaries. Miss Ryan flashed Emma an almost apologetic smile before her attention snapped back to calming the class down.

"Ok" she said loudly, "Ok now". There was no change in the volume of noise. She clapped her hands. "Ok" she repeated, obviously aware of the repetition, aware of the futility. Emma's hopes of a peaceful lesson drowning with the sound of Miss Ryan's voice.

"Ok everyone." Stop saying Ok, Emma thought crossly.

"Right!" Oh yes, much better. Emma glanced over to where Lea was sitting. She tried not to notice the way Lea raised her eyebrows at her then whispered something to Zoe, (who had the good grace to look a little sheepish and apologetic).

Then there was quiet. They looked at Miss Ryan with expectant faces. Miss Ryan was caught off guard, she hadn't formulated the words to make a sentence yet, she wasn't expecting them to be ready so soon, it normally took at least ten minutes.

"Everything alright in here, Miss Ryan?" Emma looked towards the voice and saw the real reason why the class had stopped talking. Mrs Proctor was in the doorway, blocking out the corridor behind with her great girth. Mrs Proctor was, without doubt, the largest woman, (that can still move about with surprising agility) that Emma had ever seen. Everyone feared the Proctor. She was no exception to this unspoken rule. She felt the hairs on the back of her neck stand up, the sweat wetted her underarms.

Miss Ryan cleared her throat, "Yes, thank you Mrs Proctor" she managed to say.

"Good." Mrs Proctor glared once more around the class then abruptly turned on her heels (on her precariously spindly heels – how WERE they holding up all that weight?) and stalked out of the room.

Emma stared after her. She felt embarrassed for Miss Ryan, whose eyes seemed to linger at the closing door, she looked like she almost wanted to run after Mrs Proctor, beg her to come back and help her, (take the lesson for her?) Once the door closed the class remained quiet and even Lea had turned away from Zoe to face the front of the class, her face looked bored now, apart from the odd movement of her jaw, chewing gum and, after a minute a contemptuous, over exaggerated yawn.

"Ok" Miss Ryan said. Emma immediately cringed but as Miss Ryan began to explain what the lesson would be about, pressing the computer keyboard so the powerpoint appeared with the learning objectives clearly outlined, the class were still quiet, and Emma found herself becoming more relaxed. Some of her class mates may have had expressions of disdain and, for some, blankness, but they were quiet. Miss Ryan found herself speaking more rapidly, hoping to get all she wanted to say out before they started talking amongst themselves again.

Then, there it was. A hand had been slowly raised. It was Lea. The feeling of dread returned to the pit of Emma's stomach, (did it ever go away?) Miss Ryan hadn't asked a question, she hadn't said anything that required this hand to be raised, but she couldn't ignore it any longer, she had to see what it was Lea wanted to say.

"Yes?" Miss Ryan said, her voice trying to sound nonchalant but failing to hide a slight hint of panic.

"Miss" Lea said, "Miss, I was wondering, given the way that Hitler promised all things to all people, and the way that he hid his real intentions of destroying democracy under the guise of using the system to actually gain power..." Miss Ryan's mouth dropped open a little– had she taught them this? "is it true to say then," Lea paused for dramatic effect, " that it was all so long ago that it doesn't really matter anymore?"

Miss Ryan was caught between a perverse admiration that Lea had constructed a question so succinctly and the shock of hearing her be so blatantly rude and disrespectful in front of the whole class. The class erupted into laughter and jeering, of course. The moment when Miss Ryan had felt almost in control, gone in an instant. The 'aren't I clever for ruining your lesson' look on Lea's face. Some of the class laughing hard with their noise but not with their eyes, fitting in with Lea and her group of friends, not wanting to be seen as a 'spod', 'a swot' or whatever the latest word was now for someone who actually wanted to learn. Emma just looked down at her desk. Here we go again, she thought.

3

"What's the matter, Emma?" Lea called out above the din, "You don't really think that learning about some mad man from over seventy years ago is a good use of our time?"

Emma almost dared to answer back. She, more than most, knew the true repercussions of events from the past. But how could she explain that to Lea? "Oh, by the way Lea, I have met spies who risked their lives to defeat this mad man from history, and I can tell you now, if it wasn't for them, you probably wouldn't be enjoying the freedom of speech that you are clearly demonstrating, (even if it was at the most inappropriate times!)." Thankfully, Miss Ryan found her voice at last.

"Thank you for that Lea," she said loudly, lowering the tone of her voice to get maximum volume without actually shouting and risking sounding like a shrieking fish-wife. "Perhaps you could write me an essay about your thoughts on the matter in the lunch time detention you have just earned yourself."

Lea scowled and was just about to say something when she caught the changed mood of the class. Everyone was quiet now and looked expectantly at her. However, Miss Ryan handed her the yellow detention slip. Lea just glared at her as she snatched it and stuffed it into her bag.

"Ok" Miss Ryan said, "that's enough now, as I was saying..."

Emma glanced over at Lea, but Lea was feigning interest in the lesson now, her latest outburst looking like it never happened. They used to be so close, it was so sad the way things had turned out between them.

The remaining forty-seven minutes of the lesson seem to last for at least three hours, but Emma got through it. She always got through it. It was only two lessons a week she had History with Lea. Two lessons when she sat on her own while Lea and Zoe, who used to be such good friends of hers, sat together in a huddle, laughing at her. Since the beginning of year 9, Emma had become a lot more friendly with Lucy. How could they not be close after what they'd been through together? But Lucy was in a different History class this year. It was always a relief when the bell went and Emma could meet up with her in the school canteen.

4

"How did it go today?" Lucy asked as they queued to pay for their sandwiches. She obviously heard the noises coming from Miss Ryan's class while she was in the classroom down the hall, but she didn't say so. Lucy's History teacher was Mr Evans, one of the older teachers, who had been at the school forever and yet still managed, to appear at least, to love his job. Mr Evans was good at his job, he had the magician's touch of casting a spell on a class so they respected and liked him. No talking in his lessons, no swearing, no looks of disdain. He didn't try to be funny, but he made them laugh. He had a charismatic style that could not be learned, he must have been born, fully formed with the vocation of teaching etched on his heart.

"Oh, not too bad" Emma lied, with a weak smile and busied herself with fumbling for her change to pay for her lunch. Lucy had the good grace not to question her further but Emma's heart sank a little more as they both walk out to the playground to find somewhere to sit.

Lucy and Emma still talked a lot about their wonderful secret. It was only a few months ago, at the beginning of the summer term of year 8, that they experienced, first hand, the dangers and consequences of living through the turmoil of the Second World War. They never spoke those particular words out loud, they still hadn't ever mentioned the term "time travelling", that would sound ridiculous! But what else was it? They had worked alongside Meg, a real life spy, at a crucial part of the war, the Normandy landings.

The adrenaline had faded but the feelings of excitement and the sense that they had been part of a major turning point in History hadn't. The fact that they couldn't mention it to anyone else meant that they couldn't help but relive it amongst themselves at every opportunity.

But, apart from a letter, they hadn't heard from Meg since, and both Emma and Lucy were getting worried that they would never have another adventure like their first. The letter HAD said that they might meet Meg again, but with no dates and times, Emma was getting a little impatient.

"Maybe that was it" Emma said as she took another bite of egg sandwich, "No more adventures, I mean, the War ended seventy years ago now, and there aren't many people left alive to ask about it." They were sitting on the picnic bench under the huge oak tree in the corner of the playground, on the edge of the school field.

"But the letter said…" Lucy began

"I know, but that was months ago" Emma said with her mouth full.

Lucy was half way through her sandwich. "I really can't believe that Meg would say that she'll see you again if she didn't believe it" Lucy took a bite, "She must've seen you again, or she wouldn't have said that!" she managed to say through her full mouth.

Emma frowned and tried to unscramble the sense of what Lucy had just said. "Well, I'm getting fed up waiting. I can't take much more of Lea and Zoe being so mean. Year 9 is awful so far and home is not exactly a barrel of laughs either!"

Lucy looked away. Emma realised that Lucy's home life hadn't been a barrel of laughs either and regretted her little outburst. "Sorry" she mumbled as the bell rang for afternoon lessons. "We'd better get a move on. Listen, let's go to the library after school."

By 3.15 Miss Ryan was on gate duty, making sure there wasn't any trouble as everyone barged and pushed their way out of school. She stood with her arms folded across her chest, her lanyard hidden under her coat. Her ID photo on it, a smiling and confident face rarely seen in the classroom.

"Bye Miss" Emma said as she passed her with Lucy. Miss Ryan looked up and smiled, maybe allowing herself to think that they weren't all bad.

Behind Emma, a burst of laughter as Lea and Zoe passed by – were they laughing at her? They looked so tall now they were in year 9, in their folded over skirts, showing off their long legs, intimidating to the members of the public they were streaming out of school to join. Emma walked on with Lucy. She saw Lea with a cigarette defiantly lit, well within view of the teachers on duty, Zoe on her mobile, shrieking with laughter. She noticed that Sarah was walking on her own; school is so cruel when you're not naturally one of the cool kids, Emma and Lucy should know, but at least they had each other. Emma waved shyly at Sarah as they walked down the road. There were a good number of pupils waiting outside the cafe on the corner – never too early for chips, their young, fast metabolisms burning away the fat even before they get through their own front doors for their real dinner.

"Come on, let's go to the café before the library" Emma said, grabbing Lucy's arm. If the adventure won't come to them then the café down the road was the next best thing.

Chapter One

North London, four months earlier, 2015

"Just keep your eyes open, will you?"

Emma woke with a start. What was that? She could've sworn she heard a voice. It was inky black in her room. When she opened her eyes it felt like she had a dark, velvet blindfold on. But she soon began to focus, and there was a faint glow of dawn peeping out from the bottom of her too-short curtains.

Was the voice from outside? Emma's neighbours didn't share the same sleeping patterns at all, there were always voices to be heard in the street or through the wall into next door. But the voice had seemed so close. She had felt breath on her cheek near her ear, she was sure. But how could she be sure? She had been fast asleep, hadn't she? The swirls of sleep-fugged confusion gradually began to clear and Emma sat up in bed and listened intently.

"Is someone there?" she whispered. She held her breath to see if she could hear anyone else breathing. All she could here was her own heartbeat drumming in her ears and the usual creakings of the house. Emma lived in a Victorian terraced house in London, which was never completely silent. It was like it was breathing with the effort of standing in the same spot for over a hundred years, fed up of all the door banging and chatter of its current inhabitants.

Emma lived there with her younger brother, Owen, her mum and dad and her great Nan, although when Emma had woken up she knew that her mum would be at the hospital. Nan was really poorly and mum had been there, by her side, for the past three days. Emma didn't really understand what had happened. All she knew was that

Nan was not awake yet. Awake from what, Emma wasn't told. She wasn't told a lot of stuff, she had got used to that, but it didn't stop her wondering.

"Dad? Is that you?" Emma said, a little louder this time. The shakiness she had felt when she had jerked awake was subsiding now, and she had pretty much convinced herself it had all been her imagination. Emma's eyes tracked round her room, trying to decipher the shadows, was there an outline of a person amongst the shapes? Her eyes were getting used to the faint dawn glow. She could make out her bookcase, books overflowing, with a line of stuffed toys toppling into each other along the top shelf. (Although Emma would turn thirteen next birthday she still couldn't face giving away Bunny, Panda and the rest of her comforting gang of toys.) There was her desk, with her unfinished homework seemingly reminding Emma that she would no way have time to complete it before school tomorrow. Her beanbag was slumped in the far corner, covered in her school uniform, hastily discarded the night before. There was the looming outline of her massive wardrobe, so big that it half blocked the window, and then there was her small chest of drawers next to her bed, mobile phone, ipod and clock all faintly glowing, on top. No sign of anybody at all.

She gave a big sigh and reached over to the clock, as she pressed it down she saw 5.38 flash at her, far too early to get up. She settled back down under the covers, pulling them up high, and tucking her soft rabbit under her arm. Her brain must be playing tricks on her. She was worried about her Nan and a bit worried about the unfinished homework.

"I must think of a dream" she said to herself. Her mum always gave her a dream as she kissed her at bedtime, but she hadn't been able to do that for the past three nights, of course. What would mum have said? She'd have asked what the favourite part of the day was, then made up a dream from that. As her head sunk deeper into the soft pillow, Emma thought back over the day, but all she could remember was a boring-as-usual day at school followed by a swimming lesson. "I could dream about being a mermaid and swimming down into the deep sea to hunt for treasure..." As often happened when Emma dreamt about swimming or water in general,

9

she found herself wanting to go to the toilet. She tried to ignore it and closed her eyes tighter, but she knew it was inevitable that she would get up. She was just about to fling back the covers and climb out of her cosy nest when...

There was a loud crash as something fell over. "Ouch! What is that?" the voice said. Emma thought that it was probably her guitar that she kept in its stand next to the wardrobe. But what was she thinking? Someone was in her room!

"Are you sure you haven't seen anything?" It was a woman's voice and sounded worried, and quite posh.

Emma swam back into full alert and sat bolt upright in her bed. Her rabbit fell to the floor with a loud thud.

"Who is it? Who's there?" she called out into the darkness. She brushed her untidy nest of hair back from her face with her hands, and glared as hard as she could around her room.

"I just need a bit more time and I'm sure I can find out for sure" The voice came from another part of the room, the woman was obviously pacing around. Emma heard her shoes clomping on her floorboards. "But why have I ended up here? Where, actually, am I?" the woman seemed to be talking to herself.

Emma caught a whiff of flowery perfume, the woman must have passed close by. Maybe she could've reached out to touch her if she'd timed it right.

Emma felt a strange dread creep over her, there was someone in her room for sure. But who were they? And who were they talking to? Her? Or was there a second person? Then, there it was. She could just make out a faint silhouette over on the far side of her room. Slowly, and trying not to make any fast movements to cause the someone any alarm, she reached out for her bedside lamp. This was it. She would see whoever it was in a matter of seconds. Milliseconds.

As the room burst into light, Emma gasped.

There was a young woman standing by her wardrobe, looking right at her. She can't have been much older than twenty. She was wearing bright red lipstick and had her hair curled in a complicated bun at the top of her head. She was wearing what appeared to be a dark green jumpsuit, and sensible, flat lace-ups on the woman's feet.

10

She was quite small, with bright, piercing, blue eyes and a slightly flushed face. It was a nice enough face, quite plain, but pretty and reasonably friendly-looking.

Emma took all this in in a flash because before she knew it the woman was striding across the room towards her.

"Meg" she said as she stretched out her hand, "The name's Meg", she gripped Emma's hand and shook it, hard.

Emma was too stunned to say anything. She found herself stifling a scream. A kind of squeak escaped her lips as Meg finally let go of her hand.

"And you are?" Meg said. She stood with her hands on her hips with an expectant look on her face.

A silence stretched just a little too long to be comfortable.

"Emma" Emma said eventually.

A new silence began.

"What are you doing here?" Emma managed to say at last. "How…?

Meg was pacing around the room again, in her clompy shoes. "That" she said, "is a very good question".

As Meg was about to continue, Emma managed to ask her to stop walking around in case anyone else in the house should hear, (then Emma checked herself, this woman could be dangerous, surely she *wanted* someone in the house to overhear.)

Meg looked thoughtful for a moment, as if she wasn't sure what she was going to say, then took a deep breath, " I can only presume that you are an Agent of some sort, they never tell us anything, and I know you won't be able to tell me either, so that's fine."

Emma looked blank. What on earth was this woman talking about?

"I don't want to say too much in case I've got the wrong end of the stick, you look very young for a start, and, for some reason, you're still in bed, but if I am right, and I've been sent here so you can help me then we'd better get a move on. There is a war on you know. We'll start tomorrow night" Meg stopped talking.

Emma felt the room shrink around her a little bit. A wave of confusion crashed over her, she felt very tired all of a sudden, the

11

adrenaline draining away from her. This was definitely the most real dream she had ever had in her life, but now it was getting a bit weird.

"War?" she managed to say. Meg was talking as if Britain was under threat by some war or other. Had something happened since yesterday that Emma didn't know about?

Meg looked as confused as Emma felt. "Yes, war" she said, "Why do you think I'm dressed in my Auxillary Corps uniform?" Emma looked again at the khaki green jumpsuit and a terrifying thought gripped her.

"Who's the enemy in this war?" she managed to say in a soft voice.

Meg didn't answer, she just stared at Emma with a little frown, they were both lost in their own thoughts, question upon question building up in their heads. Something had gone horribly wrong. How on earth could this have happened? Emma glanced around her room again, to make absolutely sure she was still where she thought she was. Yes, she was definitely still in her own bed, in her own room, in her own house. Meg's eyes followed Emma's, looking around the room. She took in all the furniture and toys, the books and the guitar, she also noticed some very peculiar pictures on the walls. There was a group of very moody young men dressed in leather jackets, a very sporty young woman, energetically running round an athletics track and an orang-utan with a thought bubble coming out of his head saying that it was all bananas to him. Meg almost giggled until she remembered how odd the situation was.

Emma put her head in her hands to try to compose herself. Her hair was still sticking up at all angles and her eyes felt gritty with sleep. She rubbed them vigorously to try to make sure she really was awake. In her mind, she had just formed the words of what she wanted to ask, but when she took her hands away from her face, Meg was gone.

Chapter Two

Meg had been looking out of Emma's bedroom door, into the corridor, when she'd suddenly felt a strong pull and a gust of wind. She'd closed her eyes tight, bracing herself for an impact. Was it a bomb? When she had opened her eyes she'd found herself back in her own flat. No sign of Emma, guitars or orang-utans anywhere.

Had she just fallen asleep and dreamed it all? She had been working extra shifts at the ambulance station. And with her Agency work too, she was pretty exhausted. She could easily have slept standing up. But it was too real to be a dream. She had chatted to that girl and she had felt an odd connection with her, despite the weirdness of everything.

Meg took a deep breath. She was still buzzing from what had happened. She still wasn't entirely sure how she had found herself in that unknown room. One minute she had been in her own flat, then she had opened her front door and everything had looked very odd, even in the dark. She knew she wasn't at home anymore. The first thing she noticed was the warmth – wherever she was she was leaning against a long metal heater of some sort and it was making the room really hot, not to mention her back side where she was touching it. Then the smell. It wasn't unpleasant, it just wasn't the smell of Meg's own house. It was a smell of hand cream or soap or something like that, almost like honey or boiled sweets.

The sound of gentle snoring had been coming from the other side of the room and Meg had walked over to see what creature was lurking in the corner. She was relieved to see the young girl and had known instinctively that whoever lived in that room could help her. She knew that whoever that person was it was someone that she could rely on. She hadn't known what she would say until the words had left her mouth. "Just keep your eyes open" – the first rule of her training. More important than speaking, more important than thinking itself. In any situation, just look around. Make mental notes of everything, you never know what will be useful to recall later on. Things that may seem irrelevant or mundane could hold the key to a mystery yet to be solved. Meg had got into the habit of taking imaginary photographs in her mind of any new place or situation she found herself in. The first thing she had worked out when she'd found herself in Emma's room was where all the exits were, just in case, before she had slowly worked her way around the whole room. She could still recall every detail, even the colour of Emma's duvet and the number of cuddly toys on top of her book case.

But this was getting her nowhere. Meg reached for her notebook and jotted down the key parts of what had just happened-just in case she needed to remember later on. She scratched her head with her pencil, and then scribbled something else down. Her mind wondered to what the real puzzle was – not the girl in the room but how it related to the case she was working on. Who was the one who was betraying them all? The backstabber? The traitor? The one putting the whole plan at risk? The one putting all their lives at risk?

She thought that she had whittled it down to three names. Agent Eisler (codename Rain), Agent Franklin, (codename Hail) and Agent Braun (codename Cloud), but she still wasn't certain. They were all ex-German spies, and they all knew the co-ordinates for the planned invasion of France through Normandy – the plan - Operation Neptune. The Germans knew that the Allies were coming, but they had little clue as to where they would land. If the co-ordinates were leaked, the whole operation would be ruined. The main problem with all this, of course, was that no-one could trust anyone else. As soon as you let your guard down, lives were in danger.

Meg looked out the window into the murky street below. Her flat was small, some may say pokey, but suited her well. She lived alone and could come and go as she pleased. Since the war began she had worked as an ambulance driver and then two years ago, she had been recruited to work as an Agent for MI5.

She still had to pinch herself at times. It was crazy to think of herself as some international woman of mystery –a spy! She had had to learn fast after being picked for the job by some random stranger who had recruited her in her second year at Oxford University. She must've been mad to think that she, a young twenty year old from Sleaford, a small town in Lincolnshire, would ever be able to keep state secrets and work out plans of deviousness.

Meg's particular strength had been unscrambling coded messages. She had been tested with several riddles and was the fastest to decipher what they meant. There had been some real fun ones to solve – what can travel round the world while staying in a corner? Or another one - feed me and I live, yet give me a drink and I die. No one else had got the answers to those as quick as Meg. She had shouted out "a stamp" as soon as the first question was asked and it only took her about ten more seconds to work out the answer was 'fire' to the second one. Then the messages had got more difficult – with numbers and code names, but she had studied them hard and, again, out of all the trainees, she had reached the answers first.

She had excelled at her training. She hadn't fallen for any of the traps they set up for her to see if she was trustworthy (or stupid). Sending a man to chat her up at a bus stop was particularly easy to see through. Meg had made no friends and gained a reputation as someone who would do as they were told and ask the right questions at the right time.

She had quickly risen up the ranks and was now working on this major plan based on crossing and double crossing, so complicated that if she stopped and thought about it long enough she really would lose her mind. The only way to get through it was to live, eat and breathe the plan and not get side tracked by anything silly. If this was to work (and, boy, if it worked it would end the war once and for all) she had to keep focussed. And now this had happened. A minor glitch? Or something bigger? Meg wasn't sure, but strange things had happened and she needed all her resolve and brain power to work it out before things went terribly wrong.

It was still early, not even lunch time. Meg decided to take a break from the head scratching and go and see her superior, Agent Johnson (codename Snow). He was to go on ahead to Portsmouth and be on one of the first boats to Normandy, to check over the landing sites before the masses of ships and landing gear followed. They had worked together for a long time, and, although she trusted no-one, he had never done anything to suggest he couldn't be trusted – yet.

15

They had both been responsible for turning the interned German spies onto their side. 115 or so spies had successfully been identified and caught, and most were now serving as double agents – sending false information back to the enemy – the German secret service –the Abwehr.

But now this. A double agent turned back? And Meg had to find out who, and quick. This double-crosser (or double double crosser?) had already managed to send a coded telegram back to Germany, it was a warning of what was going to happen in May. Operation Neptune had been postponed until June because of it. If the warning had been heeded the plan could be beyond salvaging already, but if the double crosser managed to make it back to Germany in person and give the co-ordinates for the landing, it would spell disaster.

Meg's thoughts returned to Emma and the latest twist in proceedings. When she'd got there she had felt compelled to ask for help but she wasn't there long enough to find out if the help was forthcoming. The puzzle of who was the traitor had reached a dead end and Meg was getting desperate. She had to solve this riddle. The most important riddle of her life. How would Emma react to being asked to help again? There was only one way to find out, she would have to try to go back tonight. How exactly Meg would do that, she wasn't entirely sure, but she would give it her best shot. But first, she needed to speak to Snow. She hadn't decided if she'd tell him everything about what had happened but she needed some fresh air, some fresh perspective. He might have more information too.

Meg put her pencil and notebook into her satchel and headed out the door.

Chapter Three

If Emma was still shaken from the goings-on from the previous night she hid it very well over breakfast. She had not really gone back to sleep after her encounter. She had searched all over for the strange woman, but found no trace. So she had got up, finished her homework and got dressed. Her head was full of Meg. She couldn't shake the feeling that this was the start of something huge. Why had Meg come into her room, and, more importantly, how? If Emma really thought about it too much she might go mad. All Emma knew was that she was excited and she couldn't wait for tonight to come to see what might happen.

Emma was tall for her age, quite skinny and had hair that needed to be tamed every morning. Her leading passion in life was music, mainly listening to it but she had begun guitar lessons now, so often pictured her future in some rock band or other. Her other great love in her life was running. She was on the school year 8 athletics team and really enjoyed the buzz and freedom of feeling the wind (and rain) beating against her as she ran like a cheetah. But her hair was one of the banes of her life. She had more time to spend on it as she was up so early but it still resembled a rather lazy, if exotic, bird's nest by the time she walked into the kitchen.

"You look dreadful, Emma, are you feeling ok?" Emma's mum asked. Emma looked up as she reached for the Rice Krispies. She felt like saying "You're a fine one to talk!" as she looked at her mum's sunken eyes, pale face and the reflection of her own wild hair, but, of course, she didn't. Her mum obviously hadn't been to bed yet and was putting a brave face on for her family. Nan must still be very poorly but Emma couldn't even think about that now, what would her mum say if she knew what had happened in her room last night. She answered her mum at last,

"I'm ok". What else do you tell your mum when you think you may have seen a ghost in your room in the early hours of the morning? Her mum wasn't really listening, Emma tried hard not to care. Her brain wasn't really processing what her mum said anyway, how could it? There was no room left in it, it was full of Meg.

"I really should get off to school anyway" Emma said. She hadn't managed even a spoonful of cereal, normally her mum would have insisted she sit down properly for 'the most important meal of the day' but her mum just said "goodbye dear". Emma kissed the top of her head and called out goodbyes to her dad and brother as she headed out the door.

Emma's mum called out a "don't forget your dinner money..." but the door had already shut.

Emma's mum was called Diana and she was tired and worried, not really knowing what to do with herself before she returned to the hospital. Great Nan was really like Diana's mother. She had raised Diana since her real mum had died when Diana was only a few days old, she even called her "ma". Despite being over 90 years old now Nan had never been really ill (or complained of being ill) all the time that she had lived with Diana and her family, and that was going on for fifteen years now.

Diana was fast falling asleep into her breakfast when her mobile on the table rang, breaking into her thoughts.

"Hello?" she answered. It was the hospital. She had to go back quickly. Great Nan, her ma, had woken up. Diana knocked the breakfast things over with a clatter as she stood up. The milk-soaked cereal spread across the table like a small advancing Rice Krispie army. It reached the sugar bowl just as the front door slammed.

School was a welcome escape at the moment for Emma. But she was so distracted on her walk there that she almost walked right passed it. She had always been a good student and was finding year 8 not particularly challenging. She could read exceptionally well, and her maths was improving. She had good friends and liked her form teacher, Miss Ross. However, year 8 was becoming a bit of a repetitive cycle of practice test after practice test. It was the last half term of the year and there would be exams soon. There was quite a lot of pressure to do well at Hitchill Street Comprehensive, but Emma wasn't one to get too stressed about exams. The walk to school did very little to clear her head. She couldn't wait to tell her best friend, Lea all about Meg.

Lea was waiting for her outside the form room. She was probably the most popular girl in year 8, she was funny and pretty and, like Emma, very good at athletics. The other pupils liked her and the teachers thought she was wonderful. Because of this, Lea could get a bit arrogant at times, but usually she could make a joke about it and all would be forgiven. She had been Emma's best friend since year two and they always looked out for each other. But could Emma tell her about last night? As Emma approached her she began to doubt if Lea would believe a single thing she said.

"You'll never guess what Lucy Kingham has gone and done, she's only gone and had her nose pierced! Miss Ross will go mad, for sure..." said Lea, enthusiastically. Emma knew it wasn't really the right time to tell her about what had happened in her room last night (what HAD happened?).

"No way!" said Emma trying to sound interested, knowing that Lea was relishing the drama of Lucy getting into trouble. There was no chance to discuss it any further though, the bell rang for the beginning of registration, they both rushed into the classroom.

"Look, there she is" Lea said in a loud whisper. Lucy didn't hear her, she had her earphones in like she always did. Miss Ross pretended not to notice most of the time, but she was looking over at Lucy now with a frown on her face.

"I can hardly watch" Lea said, with obvious delight.

"Lucy Kingham, come here please" said Miss Ross loudly, "The rest of you, get your reading books out"

Lucy unplugged herself and stuffed her earphones into her bag. To be fair to Lucy, she wasn't *really* naughty. She was just a bit different. Her uniform was a bit scruffy, she wore black eyeliner and mascara all the time and she found herself getting unreasonably angry at all the school hoops she had to jump through every day. No one from Emma's class knew her all that well (apart from Zoe who had been at primary school with her)

"What is that?" Miss Ross said, pointing at Lucy's nose ring. The class were all looking at the unfolding scene, but no one made a sound.

19

Lucy didn't say anything, she gave a slight shrug and looked down at the floor. Emma felt a bit sorry for her, but she would never say, she might get called weird as well, like Lucy so often did.

"You will go and see Mr Byron at once" Mr Byron was the head of year. He was an old, grumpy teacher who must've been working at Hitchill his whole life. He wasn't exactly scary but he never smiled and seemed to dislike children despite (or maybe because of) his job.

Lucy turned away from Miss Ross, collected her bag and walked out the classroom.

Emma didn't look at Lea. She knew that she would've been listening intently to the whole thing and be smiling at Lucy's predicament. Sometimes Lea could be such a gossip.

School passed without incident, (apart from Lucy Kingham being sent home for her nose ring) and after school, Emma found herself outside the newsagents with Lea and a few others from her class.

"Maths is so boring" Zoe was saying, "I just find it so easy, I can't be bothered with it"

"Oh you're so lucky, Zoe," said Sarah, "I can't even get the hang of my times tables let alone do fractions and you're so clever at it all"

Zoe and Sarah were kind of best friends too, but Emma suspected that Zoe was only friends with Sarah because she liked to hear all the compliments and Sarah was only friends with Zoe because she helped her with her maths all the time.

They're not best friends like Lea and I, thought Emma, but she wished that she had managed to speak to her on her own today about last night.

"Bye Emma!" called Lea as she ran off to catch up with her mum and younger sister. "See you tomorrow!"

"Bye" said Emma. Tomorrow? But tomorrow was Saturday not a school day. Of course! It was the day of Zoe's birthday party – bowling followed by a sleepover. Emma thought that she could really do without it but her mum had said it would be a welcome distraction from what was going on with Nan.

Emma trudged home, she only lived round the corner from the newsagents so it didn't take her long. The car wasn't in the drive – mum was at the hospital again.

When Diana had arrived at the now-familiar reception area of the Sparrow Ward, the nurses on duty had greeted her like an old friend.

"Hi Diana, great news! You know where to go, the doctors are just with her now," said the duty Sister. It never ceased to amaze Diana how the staff always remembered her name and who she was. There were so many doctors and nurses coming and going, changing shifts and seeing hundreds of patients every day, and yet they were so welcoming and reassuring. Diana was still anxious about everything but they had made her worries much easier to cope with. She hurried past and almost ran into the ward.

She saw her ma sitting up in the pristine, white bed almost looking like her normal self- a 90 year old version of Diana, with still thick, though very white, curly hair and bright, though surrounded by wrinkles, sparkling eyes. She was arguing with the doctor. It sounded like she was asking to leave to sort out something or other, Diana couldn't quite make out what she was saying.

"Oh ma! You're awake! How are you feeling?" Diana said. She rushed over and held her hand.

"Oh there you are dear, tell this young man that there's nothing wrong with me and I really must be getting going. I need to go now before it's too late." She seemed to be a bit confused. She wrenched her hand from Diana's grasp and tried to tug back the covers and climb out of bed.

"Just listen to the doctor, ma, he knows best" Diana was frantically tucking her in again, "and you've been unconscious for almost four days now, he needs to check you over to see if you're really ok" She exchanged glances with the doctor. They both knew that she wasn't ok.

It was the start of a long day for Diana, and the staff at the hospital. Diana would still be there arguing with her ma when Emma, her brother and her dad came to visit after school later that day.

Chapter Four

Emma had got back from the hospital quite late and dad had asked her to go straight upstairs and make sure Owen got his pyjamas on before story and bed. Owen was only two years younger than her but she always ended up being the one who was responsible for him. She could just hear the murmerings of her parents downstairs – they were obviously worried about Nan. She had been awake and looking almost back to normal when they arrived to visit, but as soon as she'd opened her mouth, they'd all known that something was wrong.

Nan had always been so 'with it'. She was the one who always suggested great days out at the weekend, she was the one who always coaxed Emma and Owen into trying new things and she was always the last one to admit that she was tired and needed to go to bed. Emma loved her Nan and it was heart breaking to see her crumbling before her very eyes. Like a once great warrior with a spear in her side. When they had seen her earlier she had been talking as if she had to be somewhere else, and she wasn't making sense. She had kept trying to get out of bed, Emma's mum had called the nurses to help her keep Nan under control and it was all really scary for Emma and Owen. Emma could make out a few snippets of conversation drifting up from downstairs.

"Well, at least she's awake, Di, that's the main thing", her dad was saying.

"But I don't want her to be awake like this!" said her mum, "if she's gone crazy, I'd rather she was unconscious again!"

"You don't mean that…" her dad's voice was drowned out by her brother's music starting up.

"Turn that off!" Emma yelled at him. She couldn't make out any more of the conversation, even leaning over the banister. Emma contemplated going downstairs to see if she could find out more, but she knew that her mum and dad wouldn't carry on if she were there. Emma walked back into her room, put her own music on and checked her phone. A message from Lea asking her what she was going to wear for Zoe's bowling party tomorrow. She chucked the phone on her bed, it didn't seem right that normal life was still going on when things were so different at home. The next song came on – 'Scream out loud', one of Emma's favourites and just what she felt like doing.

However, Emma felt quite excited when she got into bed later. Would she have the same dream as last night? Because that must've been what had happened, there really was no other explanation. Emma had convinced herself that was what it was anyway. It was still a good dream though and she desperately hoped she could remember the details to pick up where she left off – Emma knew how hard it was to remember dreams but this one was still quite clear – even the shade of lipstick the woman had been wearing.

Her mum came to give her a kiss goodnight. "What was your favourite part of the day?" Diana asked. She always asked Emma this so she would have something nice to dream about.

"Um, I s'pose PE was quite good today" Emma said, a little desperately, she didn't want to mention the hospital visit, Diana looked too tired to talk about Nan any more.

"Ok," said Diana, "here's a dream…" and she outlined a fantastical PE lesson full of trampoline acrobatics and flying tennis matches. Emma found herself giggling, despite the sombre mood of the evening. Her mum always made her feel better, and like things would be alright in the end.

"Night night" Diana kissed Emma's forehead, "Don't read too late"

"Night mum, I won't" Emma settled down with her school reading book without taking much of it in. Five minutes later she turned off her lamp and closed her eyes tight.

Come on, sleep she thought to herself, come on. Emma tried to think about last night and what she had done to make the woman appear, but she didn't think she'd done anything different to normal. She tried thinking of the dream her mum had given her and was just beginning to drift off into the world of PE teachers who were really circus performers when she heard a rustling sound. She definitely wasn't asleep yet.

"Hello?" she called out, "Anyone there?" She felt a tingle of excitement.

The rustling stopped. "Hello?" she said in a loud whisper. Doubt enveloped her like an unwelcome blanket.

But she didn't have to wait long for a reply, and it wasn't nearly as scary because she had half expected it. It was still totally weird though.

"Ah, there you are, I was wondering whether you'd be here again, well, no time to lose, we'd better get going" The voice reached Emma before she could make out Meg striding towards her across the room. There she was again, the woman from the night before now in a smart blue dress, curled hair and bright red lipstick. She looked oddly out of place next to the poster-clad walls of Emma's room.

"W-where are we going?" Emma stammered. She found herself getting out of bed and putting on her slippers and dressing gown. "Should I change?"

"I'll explain on the way" the woman replied briskly. "I really haven't got time now, time is of the essence, yes? You look fine in what you've got on" she looked doubtfully at Emma's dark blue dressing gown, it could pass for a coat, in bad light.

Emma liked the way she spoke, in posh, clipped tones, but she really didn't know why "time was of the essence", she supposed that she'd have to follow her and find out why. She didn't feel frightened but she was worried what her mum would say if she saw what she was about to do. But then again, Emma reasoned to herself, it would only add to her worries so she thought maybe she would be better just to go, and explain later.

Emma and Meg stepped through the bedroom door. A cold rush of air nearly took Emma's breath away. Where was her landing? Instead, there was a dark street. Emma gasped but Meg was already marching off into the murk. Emma rushed after her, where in the world was she? What on earth was she doing? Would she ever get home? "Wait!" She called. "What on earth is going on? Where are we?"

"I know, I found it a bit weird the first time I stepped through whatever it is we just stepped through," said Meg, quite matter-offactly, "You'll soon get used to it. Now, do keep up and I'll try to explain what's going on." Meg barely drew breath. "We have to work quickly. There may be a cloud in the sky and it looks like rain may be on its way." She gave Emma a quick sideways glance to see if this statement, apparently about the weather, got any reaction.

Nothing. Emma was concentrating on keeping up and not walking into anything, it was so very dark. She could hear what Meg was saying but hadn't a clue why she was discussing the weather when she was acting with such urgency. The street looked vaguely familiar but it was not light enough to see properly. And the smell? It smelled of smoke and burning but there were no obvious fires anywhere that Emma could see.

Meg carried on. "If we get to the Lyons tea shop before rain then we might be able to sit nearby and, you know?"

"Not get wet?" Emma ventured.

"Exactly!" said Meg, somewhat pleased. Emma must've said the right thing. Emma wasn't sure why. It was only logical that if they were indoors they wouldn't get wet, but she had a feeling Meg meant something entirely different. Well, it was too late to ask now, just as she opened her mouth to clarify, Meg stopped abruptly outside a building with all its blinds drawn.

"Here we are!" She said. "Now remember, eyes, and especially ears, open." She hustled Emma into the building, the tea shop, as it turned out, and they found a table in the corner to squeeze into.

The café wasn't quite full and Emma could get a good view of all the other customers as she sat with Meg. Everyone looked like they were on the set of a film. There were men in uniform, some speaking in loud American accents. There were some beautiful women nearby, all with bright red lips like Meg, and many smoking thin cigarettes. No smoking ban here then, Emma thought to herself. She checked herself, what was she thinking? Smoking or not smoking was the last thing she should be worried about. What was she doing here? Where in the world was she? Or should that be when?

As the silence wore on Emma felt the need to say something, she'd never liked silence and felt quite embarrassed, as if she should really be the one to speak up.

"What exactly are we…"

But she never got to finish her sentence, Meg silenced her with a firm "shhh" as the door of the café opened and a tall, elegant woman walked in. She nodded, almost unperceptively, towards Meg and then sat down next to an equally elegant looking man.

Emma thought that they looked like film stars. They sat facing each other, not saying much but their legs were almost touching, they looked close. A harassed looking waiter, with a black apron tied round his waist, brought over a pot of tea and two cups. Emma didn't see them order, they must come here a lot and have a regular order, she thought.

"What do you see?" Meg said in a whisper.

Emma wasn't sure what was required from her. She looked round the café. There were tables crammed into every available space, some with flowery table cloths and some in various shades of gingham. She saw men dressed in uniforms, and some women too. Everyone seemed to be smoking and there was some quiet, piano music playing from a radio somewhere. "I see a man and a woman having tea together" she said. Was that the right answer? She really wanted it to be, she desperately wanted to impress Meg, and wasn't sure why it mattered so much.

"Look again" said Meg, as she took something out of her satchel. Cigarettes? Surely she wasn't going to smoke near her, a child, thought Emma.

Emma pretended to scratch her ear as she turned round to look at the couple again. As she looked she saw the man deliberately knock his tea over and it spilled onto the woman's lap forcing her to stand up and shout quite loudly. The waiter rushed over and began mopping wildly at the woman's skirt with a napkin, which only made the woman shout louder. She grabbed the napkin and tried to mop up the drink herself. Most people in the café had turned to look at the couple, who were now really arguing. Emma looked back at Meg. She was the only one whose attention was not on the rowing couple.

Instead, she was looking just beyond them to the back of the café where a door was just swinging shut.

"Classic" Meg said under her breath. "Come on, we have to go" she left a few coins on the table and Emma followed her out, leaving the chaotic scene behind them.

"You've got to do better than that" Meg said to Emma when they got outside, "I don't know why Snow has sent me such an amateur". She set off walking in the direction where they had come from earlier.

Emma, not for the first time that evening, felt embarrassed and unsure of what was expected of her. She didn't know where she was, she didn't know how she had got there, she didn't' know who she was with. Emma felt a flash of anger, how dare this woman criticise her? She didn't ask to come here. She felt a bit scared that she'd come along with this strange woman. What was she thinking? What would her mum say when she told her? (Would she tell her?)

"What do you mean?" said Emma, pulling her dressing gown tighter round her waist, "I don't even know why I'm here" Meg stopped and turned round forcing Emma to come to an abrupt halt too.

"The man? In the café?" Meg said, "You didn't even notice him"

"I did" Emma said indignantly, "I was looking at him as he deliberately poured the tea on that woman, I saw it happen, he did it on purpose".

"Not that man" Meg said, "The one who was sitting just behind, the one who sneaked out the back of the café just as everyone's eyes were on the so-called arguing couple, the one who dropped this note on the floor by my satchel" Meg held a piece of paper in her hand that Emma couldn't quite read.

Emma cast her mind back to the scene. Was there another man? She couldn't be sure. She suddenly felt stupid, and a bit tearful, and quite cross.

"Who are you anyway?" she said with a crack in her voice, " I didn't ask to come with you, I don't even know what we're doing. All this weird talk about time being of the essence, it's not even raining! Could you just take me home please? It's cold and dark and I have to go to a party tomorrow, not that I really want to, it's just I promised a friend, and now I'm going to be tired and confused and I just want to go home." Emma was panicking. She was scared now, where was she? Why on earth had she followed this stranger to wherever it was they were.

Meg looked a little aghast at Emma for her outburst. She knew that she would have to tell Emma a bit more information or she would be of no help at all. "You know I can't tell you everything but I think I'd better tell you what our mission actually is."

"Mission?" said Emma, she felt a dread creep over her. This was sounding like a James Bond film.

"I work for Agent Snow" Meg continued, "he has told me that one of our double agents has turned. They are all ex German spies. It could be Rain, it could be Hail or it could be Cloud. They are trying to stop Operation Neptune"

Emma must've looked blank, so Meg expanded a bit more. "We are planning to start the liberation of France. Those poor people have been occupied by the Germans for pretty much the entire war, living under German rule, in constant fear. We are going to launch a land, sea and air invasion to set them free – this could be the beginning of the end of the war, Emma, I'm telling you, it's vital the plan goes ahead." She paused to let go of Emma's arm that she'd just grabbed. "We are arriving in Normandy to take the Germans by surprise. It is crucial that the Germans don't know where the landings are going to happen. This traitor who I need to find has the exact co-ordinates of the invasion. If he tells the Germans, all is lost. They will be waiting for us and the advantage of surprise is gone. We will most probably fail."

Emma tried to take all this in. She knew a little bit of history about the War, but this was a lot to process.

"Rain was the one who just dropped the note in my bag." Meg said. She waited for Emma's reaction.

It was Emma's turn to look slightly aghast. "I, I , I don't really think I know what you're…"

Meg interrupted her, It's getting late, come with me" she said, and led Emma into a doorway. "In there"

Emma hesitated, she didn't want to leave it like this but she really wanted to be alone to sort out in her head what she had just heard.

"Go on, It'll be fine, I'll see you tomorrow" said Meg.

Emma opened the door and walked into her room. The cold air, she was home.

Chapter Five

Meg woke up the next day with her head full of the night before. She unfolded the piece of paper that Rain had given her last night.

Cirrus can change colour and is climbing higher

It wasn't the first time she had received a coded note, it came with the job, but she was feeling really flummoxed about this one. She took a drag from her cigarette, stubbed it out and looked at the note again.

Her thoughts were interrupted by a knocking at the door. That would be Florrie coming to call for her. They were on duty at the ambulance station in half an hour. "Coming!" Meg called.

Meg volunteered for the Women's Army Auxillary Corps. She'd had her driving licence for about a year and enjoyed the challenge of driving the ambulances through the bombed out streets. She'd seen some horrific sights and had to carry both alive and dead passengers throughout the shifts she worked. But she felt her job was vital – not only to the war effort but also to throw anyone off the scent of her other job.

What did the note mean? She'd have to ask Rain next time she saw him, but how could she trust him? He was one of the agents she was investigating. Trust your instincts Meg, she thought to herself, that's all I have.

The knocking sounded on the door again, "Alright!" Meg called. She splashed cold water on her face on her way out past the communal bathroom and ran down the stairs to the front door.

The ambulance shift was a hard one that day. The morning was spent transferring patients from their homes (well, temporary homes-most of the patients had lost their homes during the bombings) to the hospital for check ups and the removal of plasters from broken limbs. The amount of air raids had lessened as the war years had gone on but the Luftwaffe still came and when they did, the damage was shocking. There were also lots of injuries caused from the black outs every night from people falling over and into things, and all the new jobs that had been created often threw up the odd casualty too, especially in the dangerous munition factories.

During Meg's lunch break she tried to sneak out to contact Rain about the note. She was just heading out to the phone box when Mr Soloman, the head of their ambulance unit, marched over to them – a building had collapsed in Walthamstow – Florrie and Meg were needed.

"I hope it's not too dreadful today, I have a date later and I don't want to be worn out otherwise I won't have enough energy to dance" Florrie said with a whine. Meg was driving out of the depot, heading east.

"Jimmy?" Meg asked.

"No, no no, Jimmy was last week, he had to go, he was getting too serious, no, it's Will tonight, he's from America you know." Florrie said proudly. Florrie was gorgeous in an obvious sort of way, peroxide blonde hair and bright red lips, she thought of herself as Jean Harlow in *Reckless,* she continued talking about the wonderful qualities that American soldiers have over British ones, but Meg had already lost interest and was concentrating on the journey in hand. The usual way to Walthamstow was blocked so she had to drive the long way round, but at least she had time to think about the note - *Cirrus can change colour and is climbing higher.*

Right, Cirrus? The possibilities? A person's name? Italian? Greek? A Greek god? Or an object? Something that can change colour? AND climb high. A balloon? That can't change colour. Does climbing higher mean a literal climb? Doubtful, it's code, Meg, think. Meg always had these internal arguments with herself and thrashing it out like this normally helped, but she was drawing a blank today. Think Meg! Climbing high – the top of a building? A room up high? A hill? A mountain??

She was getting nowhere.

"Are you listening to me?" Florrie said, with a shake of her magnificent hair, and her best sulky pout.

"Yes, of course I am" Meg said, a little abruptly as her thoughts melted into thin air

"I said, did you hear about Molly?" Florrie said, "She's getting really friendly with Dereck, you know? The ambulance station manager, she fancies herself for a promotion I think, a real social climber she is, reckons she's a real high flier…"

"What did you just say?" Meg asked excitedly, she had a sudden thought.

"Molly, she is going for a promotion"

"No, not that bit, the other bit" Meg said

"She's a social climber? A high flier?" Florrie looked a little confused, as if this was the least important part of the conversation. She liked Meg but thought her a bit vague and distant. Maybe she wasn't very successful with the boys like Florrie was and that's why she was never really interested in Florrie's conquests.

"Thank you, Florrie" Meg said quietly. She smiled to herself. The first half of the coded note solved, so she thought – climbing higher might mean someone is seeking promotion of their own or at least talking to someone high up. Maybe this Cirrus is talking to someone about Operation Neptune? Operation Neptune that was in danger of being jeopardised, where a traitor's words could ruin everything? Was Cirrus the traitor? Meg vowed to find out exactly who this Cirrus was, and fast.

"Meg? What is it?" Florrie asked, "Is it a fella?" Florrie was always trying to fix Meg up with someone or other, maybe she had been wrong and Meg was a real firecracker with the fellas!

"Kind of" said Meg, not untruthfully.

Florrie gave a shriek, "I knew it" she said, "Who is he? We can double date? Is he a soldier? Of course he is, you wouldn't go with no conchie, what does he look like? Bet he's really handsome…" Florrie rambled on, answering her own questions, as they drove into Walthamstow.

Chapter Six

Emma had woken up that morning knowing that her meeting with Meg had not been a dream – she could almost smell the cigarette smoke from the café still. She sat up slowly, she could hear the breakfast noises from downstairs and willed herself to get up.

Diana was setting out the bowls for cereal when Emma walked into the kitchen. "Ah, there you are, Cheerios or Rice krispies?" Diana said, "And do you want to pop with me to the hospital before Zoe's party this afternoon?

Emma didn't really feel like going to see her Nan OR going to Zoe's party but she found herself feeling guilty and saying yes before sitting down for breakfast. It can't be easy for mum, Emma thought, and she's always so upbeat and non-complaining. She had a lot on her plate, but Emma needed to get some advice on all this stuff that was going on. Emma opened her mouth to speak,

"Mum?" She said, "have you ever…"

But she didn't get a chance to finish her sentence, Owen came bounding in with Emma's dad and started asking for toast and marmite and "make it quick" as he had football practise starting in 15 minutes. Brothers were so annoying.

Zoe's party was at 3pm and Emma arrived there, parcel in hand, just as everyone was putting on the, slightly warm, bowling shoes.

"Emma!" Zoe said loudly, as she rushed over to air kiss her, "Mwah! Mwah!" Zoe was wearing a sparkly t-shirt and her pink, skinny jeans. Her black, curly hair was pulled into complicated corn rows as usual and her voice was as loud as ever.

"Happy Birthday, Zoe! – here" Emma thrust the parcel into Zoe's eager hands. Emma felt less glamorous than Zoe, as always. Emma was wearing her usual uniform of black leggings and band-logoed t-shirt. Her wild hair had been cajoled into a pony tail of sorts but was making a bid to escape the scrunchy already.

Emma liked Zoe but, while she was looking forward to the bowling, she wasn't feeling the same about the sleepover later. She'd hoped that her mum would have said no, because of Nan and everything, but her mum seemed glad that Emma was carrying on with her life as usual, and had urged her to have fun. Emma hated sleeping anywhere but home, she often felt a little homesick on sleepovers and that was before being visited by Meg. What if Meg came tonight when she wasn't there? Would she find her at Zoe's?

"Come on, Em, let's get some drinks before we bowl" Lea had appeared and dragged Emma off to the café part of the bowling centre. Lea was looking as sparkly as Zoe, her straight blonde hair held back tastefully in an Alice band and a light blue jumper of just the right colour as to show off her eyes to maximum effect. Lea was as polished as a diamond and she knew it.

"You'll never guess who's here", Lea said, with her usual gossipy tone. She didn't give Emma a chance to answer with a list of possibilities, "Lucy Kingham!" she said with a flourish. Emma wasn't that surprised actually, she knew that Zoe had known Lucy since they were babies and their families lived next door to each other. She also knew that Zoe didn't particularly like Lucy any more, she had called her unpredictable and weird. Lucy was always getting into trouble at school and she didn't seem to have any friends of her own. But Zoe could be kind, and she obviously invited Lucy because she thought it would be a nice thing to do, (and to show off her bowling skills, of course!)

Bowling was fun – but Zoe had insisted on no gutter supports so Emma found that the balls she bowled often didn't reach the intended target of the ten pins. Zoe obviously won – her dad had bowled for the county when he was younger and she had spent a lot of time watching him bowl and practising. Oh well! It was her birthday – she's allowed to gloat annoyingly at her victory, thought Emma.

"Well done, Lucy" Emma said kindly as the girls took their seats for the after bowling food. "You nearly got a strike on that last go".

Lucy shrugged and stared determinedly into her Diet Coke.

"What happened to your nose ring?" Emma was trying to get Lucy to be more involved in the party chat. Emma knew that she had been sent home for it, of course, and now it had been taken out.

Lucy touched her nose, self -consciously, and shrugged again. She didn't really speak much at the best of times. Everyone thought she was either really rude, or painfully shy, and yet, at school, she was always saying the wrong thing in front of the teachers and getting into terrible trouble. Emma just thought she was shy, she liked Lucy and, secretly, thought she was pretty cool. The black eye make- up, the Doctor Martin boots, the ripped denim mini skirt – she looked like some sort of rock star.

"Happy Birthday to you! Happy Birthday to you! Happy Birthday dear Zoe, Happy Birthday to you!" The cake arrived with the thirteen candles burning brightly and Zoe made a big show of blowing them all out in one go. Everyone clapped and even Lucy seemed to brighten as the cake was cut up and everyone had a slice. Emma was enjoying herself, she really did have some good friends – Zoe, Lea, and Sarah was there as well, and Lucy was alright too. Maybe the sleepover would be ok after all.

"Now girls, I know there's no use saying go to bed at 10, but at least try to keep the noise down" said Zoe's mum as she was leaving a floorful of girls in her daughter's bedroom.

"Yes Mrs Lucas" the girls all chorused, giggling. They'd all got changed into their pyjamas and onesies ages ago and watched a dvd while painting each other's toe nails startling shades of pink, purple and red.

"Night Night then" Mrs Lucas called as she shut the bedroom door.

"I thought she'd never leave!" said Zoe in a loud whisper. "Right, who's for a game of truth or dare?" She looked round at her friends, expectantly.

Lea groaned, "Really, Zoe, truth or dare is such a cliché ," Zoe's face fell, " what about secret or dare where everyone has to tell us a secret or take on a dare?"

Lea could be very bossy sometimes but Zoe didn't seem to mind, her face lit up again, "Ok" she said, "Lea, tell us a secret!"

Lea looked thoughtful, but it was obvious that she was bursting to tell the secret she had in mind. "Well, "she said, "I saw Miss Enstone mouthing 'call me' to Mr Green at break yesterday and he nodded and gave her a wink!"

"No! Really?" came the exclamations from everyone else. Only Lucy looked unimpressed. "Ahh! They'd make a lovely couple" said Sarah.

"Yuck! That's gross!" said Zoe, "he must be at least 30! And she's so young and pretty"

The conversation turned to which teachers' were pretty and which were old, until Lea interrupted and got everyone back on track with the game.

"Lucy" She said, "Secret or dare?" Lucy looked a little startled and went bright red. "Um, dare I think, I don't really know any secrets" she said.

Lea squealed with delight as she revealed the dare that she'd obviously had in mind when she'd thought the game up in the first place. "Go into Zoe's brother's room and steal something!"

Zoe's brother was 17 and his bedroom was opposite her room. Even Zoe looked a bit concerned at this dare.

"I don't think that would be a good idea" she said. "Ben is seriously grumpy these days and if he knows someone's been in his room he will kill me for sure"

"He's not in there now, is he?" said Lea.

"Well, no but…"

"Well there you go then. Go on Lucy, or you'll have to tell us a secret, that's the rules of the game" Lea was determined that the girls stick to the rules.

Lucy looked stricken and didn't look like she was going to move from inside her sleeping bag on Zoe's floor. There was a moment of tension before she suddenly leapt up and said "ok then" as she walked out of the room.

"She's not really going to, is she?" Emma said.

Everyone scrambled to the door and looked out as Lucy disappeared into Ben's room opposite. She appeared a few seconds later holding what looked like a rugby sock. She tossed it into Zoe's room.

"Ugh! Smelly sock!" Lea said with a squeal. She threw it at Emma.

"Argh! Not at me!" Emma threw it quickly into the air. It landed near Sarah who was almost hyperventilating with giggles. "Getitoffme!" she said, the sock was thrown again.

The sock throwing continued and everyone had a turn at screaming and pretending to be horrified. Well, nearly everyone. Lucy stood just out of the action, halfway in the hallway with an unreadable expression on her face. Emma noticed this and was puzzled why Lucy didn't join in. But there was no time to think about that now, a smelly rugby sock had just landed on her shoulder.

Meg was still puzzling over the coded message when she finished her shift later on that evening. The Black Out was already in place as she walked back home to her shared flat and she took the little torch out of her bag. As she walked through her front door a big blast of wind blew right into her face forcing her eyes shut. A bomb? She hardly dare look. When she opened her eyes again, she had to blink a few times before she could focus on what was in front of her.

A dark room. A dark room with what looked like dead bodies on the floor lying perfectly still. Were they dead? Was she? To her relief one of the "bodies" rolled over and let out a huge fart. Not dead then, just asleep, but Meg was wondering how she had got there. She got the torch out again and she shone it around the room. She could make out a few pictures on the walls, pictures of young men with longish hair, strange clothes and pouting faces. She could also see lots of cuddly toys and a desk piled high with books. She heard a noise and whipped her head round to see a familiar sleeping face – Emma. So that was why she was here. Emma must be able to help her with the message. Meg stepped over another sleeping girl and whispered close to Emma's ear.

"Emma? Emma? Wake up!" she said in a loud whisper.

Emma stirred, but flicked Meg away with her hand and rolled over.

"Emma, wake up this instant, it's me, Meg"

Emma's eyes shot open, it only took a second for her brain to catch up and to realise who was there. "Meg? What are you doing here? How did you find me?" Her heart was thumping in her chest now. What would happen if anyone woke up and saw a strange woman talking to her?

"I don't really know" said Meg, truthfully, "I was just coming home from my shift and I opened the door and…"

"Shhhh!" Emma said, sharply as Lucy stirred next to her. There was a couple of moments before she spoke again, making sure she lent close to Meg and Lucy was still asleep, "I can't come with you, I'm at a sleepover. This is my friend, Zoe's house. If they wake up and I'm not here they'll be so worried, I'm sorry, you're going to have to go, come back when I'm at home."

Meg shone her torch over the other sleeping girls. She nodded that she understood and walked towards the bedroom door. Emma watched her go with mounting disappointment. She desperately wanted to talk to Meg but she couldn't risk Zoe or any of the others finding out.

But when Meg stepped outside she found herself in an unfamiliar corridor. She was not back in her flat at all. She really didn't know how she was going to back. Maybe she could only get back once Emma had helped her? She peered into the room opposite the one she'd just come out of. As she peeked in the door a horrible smell hit her – maybe some sort of animal lived in there? She stood back in the middle of the corridor and tried to think what to do. She was obviously sent here for a reason, she'd have to go back into Zoe's room and get Emma.

"Emma? "Emma?" Emma was still where Meg had left her five minutes ago, sitting up in a sort of daze. "I can't get back, I think I need your help before I can leave" Meg said in another loud whisper. Emma looked round at her sleeping friends. She felt that tingle of excitement again. "Come on," she said, "Let's go downstairs, we can talk there". Meg and Emma crept out of the room and tiptoed down the stairs.

Once they got into Zoe's living room they could talk more freely, but it was weird for both of them. The room itself opened up at the bottom of the stairs. It was a dining room as well as a living room and decorated in the usual magnolia of all the houses Emma ever visited. It had a massive leather sofa pointing at one wall where there hung the biggest screen Meg had ever seen. The floor was laminate and so they both had to tiptoe over to the table and chairs at the far end of the room. Neither could sit down though. Meg paced

38

up and down and Emma kept glancing nervously towards the stairs, convinced that Zoe's parents would be down in any minute. How would she explain this one to them?

"Right", said Meg, trying to get back her brisk and business- like manner again, but she was a little taken aback by the situation, to say the least. "I think the reason I'm here is because of this coded message I got from last night, you know, when we were in the tea house?"

Emma remembered the café, of course, she still felt embarrassed about missing whatever it was that Meg had seen and she hadn't. "Ok" Emma said, uncertainly, "What message?" Meg handed Emma the note, *Cirrus can change colour and is climbing higher.*

"Any ideas?" Meg said. She anxiously nibbled at her already well-bitten nails.

"None" said Emma, truthfully, "Who's Cirrus?"

"That's the problem," said Meg, "I've no idea, it's not a surname or a code name I recognise. Emma looked thoughtful. It was still taking a while for the sleep fog to leave the brain. She looked around the room for any ideas.

"What's your code name?" she asked, she just felt curious, it wouldn't help what they were talking about.

"Sunshine" said Meg with a little smile.

Emma smiled too, "That's nice" she said, and thought that it sounded a lot better than Hail or Thunder or whatever the others were called. She noticed the laptop in the corner of the room. Surely it was worth doing an internet search on "Cirrus"?

"Let's check the internet" Emma said, and walked over to the computer, she lifted the lid and the screen lit up.

Meg looked blank, "The inter- what?" she said.

"You know, let's do a google search, see if Cirrus comes up" Emma said, with a frown. Why didn't Meg know what she was talking about? Meg's expression didn't change. An uneasy feeling crept up on Emma. Meg must be from another planet not to know what the internet was. Another planet or another time? Emma knew her thoughts were crazy but it wasn't the first time she had had them. She shook her head as if to shake the thoughts away, at least for the time being.

"Enter your passcode" Emma read out loud. Meg had come over to marvel at the computer. Her face glowed in front of the screen and reflected her amazed expression. What was this? She understood the words on the screen but how had they appeared? There were no wires to be seen anywhere. Emma was frowning again, she typed in a few numbers and the screen changed to clear blue surrounded by little square symbols.

"Most people can't be bothered to think up a passcode" she said, "they just use 1,2,3,4, it's easier to remember."

Meg looked impressed. "Are you sure you haven't been to Bletchley?" she asked.

Emma didn't know what Bletchley was so just gave Meg a funny look before turning her attention back to the screen.

Did Emma understand more about codebreaking than she let on? Meg thought, maybe she really was a spy? She was very good at pretending not to be.

Emma was tapping in some more code now. Meg could see the word "Cirrus" appearing in a long box. Emma pressed search and turned to Meg. "It's a type of cloud" she said.

"What?" said Meg, still staring at the screen.

"Cirrus", said Emma, "it's a type of cloud" She continued to read, "they form above 20,000 feet. In the day time, they are whiter than any other cloud in the sky. While the sun is setting or rising, they may take on the colours of the sunset."

Meg's mind was whirring, "Agent Cloud!" she said suddenly, "It has to be. But is he climbing high? Talking to someone high up? On whose side? Has he changed colour? Switched allegiance?" Meg paused. "It was Agent Rain who gave me that note." She stopped again. She was nearly there, she could feel it. Think Meg, think, she willed herself to get it.

There was silence in the living room as both Meg and Emma were lost in their own theories about the coded message. Emma broke the silence first. "You said Agent Rain gave you the note?" She said.

"That's right" said Meg, it was her turn to frown now.

Emma went on "So Agent Rain has basically told you that Agent Cloud has been talking to people high up about something and he may have changed sides."

Meg let that idea sink in. It was what she had been thinking too but it was really hard to know if that really was what Rain had meant and if he had, was he telling the truth?

A door opening upstairs broke into both their thoughts. "Emma" came a loud voice, "Are you down there?" It sounded like Lucy.

"You'll have to go" Emma said quickly to Meg. "Just getting a glass of water" she called up the stairs. Meg was already heading towards the door. She hoped that it would open back to her own flat. She didn't have time to worry though, or say goodbye to Emma, she opened the door and smelt a familiar smell. She was home.

Chapter Seven

Meg looked around her familiar flat and felt a sense of relief at being back but also a sense of dread at what she thought she had found out. She would have to talk to Rain. If it was true and Cloud had switched sides then they would have to move fast. She knew that all the spies that she had helped recruit to become double agents carried the risk of returning to the enemy but none that she had known of, and none that had seemingly turned back at such a crucial time. Operation Neptune was so close now. The paratroopers were briefed and ready, the RAF, the Navy, the army- all being co-ordinated to the minutest detail. Nothing should be slowed to jeopardise the plan.

Meg headed out into the darkness and got out her torch again, she was heading back to Lyons, maybe Rain was there again. She walked as fast as the blackout would allow her without tumbling over. But she hadn't got very far when the familiar sound of the sirens started up. Air Raid wardens appeared and ushered her into the nearest underground station.

It wasn't very busy, at this time of night most people were in their own Anderson shelters in their own gardens. Meg knew she would have to abandon seeing Rain tonight. She grabbed a cup of tea from the volunteers and settled down onto the platform. As she kicked off her shoes and gratefully accepted a blanket that was proffered to her she gazed around at her fellow bed-mates. She still wasn't used to seeing the little hammocks strung across the tracks and couldn't help imagine the horror of what was going on above her head as the faint noise of bombs being dropped started.

There didn't seem to be much of a gap between the bangs from above tonight. It was relentless and Meg didn't get a chance to sleep at all. She remembered when she'd been in Balham station at the beginning of the war and a bomb had blown a hole in the road overhead. A bus had fallen into the crater and damaged the station below, bursting pipes along the way. The flooding and mayhem that followed had killed nearly seventy people. The underground was safer than being out and about, but Meg always found herself thinking of those poor souls back in 1940.

She found herself next to a very chatty (just frightened?) young woman who took Meg's mind off disaster and prattled on about her husband and how he was giving as good as we were getting tonight over the skies of some poor German city at this very moment. Meg vaguely wondered if the German civilians were cowering in their shelters just like she was. It was going to be a long night.

Diana came to pick Emma up from Zoe's just before 11 the following morning. She found a very grumpy, tired girl who was in no mood to talk about the sleepover, the party or anything really. So Diana just talked at her as Emma stared out of the car window.

"Nan was sitting up yesterday afternoon, and talking quite normally for a change" Diana said, "She asked after you and Owen and chatted about the weather. I really think she's over the worst of it."

Emma made some noise of being pleased to hear this, she knew what her mum was going to say next even before the car turned away from home towards the hospital. "Let's just pop in to see her on the way home" Diana said, "Dad and Owen are there already so we have to pick them up anyway".

Emma was too tired to argue. Her brain was feeling exhausted from thinking of Meg's visit last night and her body ached from spending all night on the floor in Zoe's room. She hoped Meg had told whoever she had to tell about the cracked message – *had* they cracked the message? There was no time to think about that now, they were entering the hospital car park and she really should get into great grandchild-mode.

Nan was sitting up when Emma and her mum walked into the ward. Emma's dad, Richard, was reading aloud from the local newspaper and Owen was helping himself to the grapes on the bedside table.

"Yes, it says here that the police haven't caught the culprit yet, but they've assured Mr Broughton that his bike will be found within the week. Ahh! Di, there you are" Emma's dad looked relieved as Emma and her mum approached.

"Hi ma!" Diana said in that loud clear voice used for talking to old deaf people, "I've brought Emma to see you". She pushed Emma gently towards the bed.

"Hello Nan" Emma said. She found that she was pleased to see her great Nan looking so well after only hearing the bad news about her from her parents.

"Emma, dear" Nan said, "Did you have fun last night? Everything sorted?" Emma glanced at her mum for any clue as to what that meant but Diana just raised her eyebrows and nodded encouragement.

"The weather seems so much clearer now, don't you think?" she continued, "dry and bright and hardly a cloud in the sky". Emma looked out of the window and nodded in agreement, although it was very grey outside and had just begun to rain. Emma's dad made the universal sign for *she's crazy* by whirling his forefinger in a circle by the side of his head.

"I can see that, Richard" Nan said suddenly. Emma felt a laugh escape as her dad went red with embarrassment. "He doesn't know a thing, does he?" Nan said with a wink.

Emma was confused but felt an odd feeling of comfort settle on her shoulders. Did Nan know something about Meg? How? Is that what happened to your brain when you got old and crazy? Maybe Emma was going crazy? How else could she see Meg? She had never really questioned where Meg came from but she knew it wasn't' where she was from (or when).

The rest of the visit passed with various comments about the doctors not knowing anything and how fine Nan felt and how well Emma and Owen were doing at school. Richard continued to make the odd gaff before Diana finally noticed that Emma could barely keep her eyes open and it was time to go home.

"Bye Nan" Emma lent over to give her a kiss. She smelled of lavender soap as always and her skin was so soft and paper thin. As Emma pulled away her granny gripped her arm, "just keep your eyes open, dear" she said in an urgent whisper.

Emma was caught off guard. She walked towards the exit. She felt she should say something but as she turned to walk back, she saw that the old lady had fallen asleep. Just a coincidence then? Or did she know that was the first thing Meg had ever said to her? Emma wasn't sure. Yet another thing to ask Meg tonight.

Sunday afternoon passed without any more drama, unless you call doing maths homework dramatic! As bedtime approached Emma felt more and more excited and less and less tired. She was glad to get into her room after tea. She didn't change into her pyjamas this time, just in case. As she pulled back her duvet to climb in and read, she found a square of paper neatly folded. Emma's heart beat quickened as she carefully opened it.

"It's on for tonight, be ready" Emma read it out loud. Her heart showed no sign of slowing down. Meg would be coming again tonight and she needed to be ready. For what? Emma could hardly wait to find out.

Chapter Eight

"Oh, there you are, come along, I've got another message" Meg hadn't come into Emma's room as expected, and Emma had got a bit worried that she wasn't coming at all. But as Emma went to the bathroom to brush her teeth the cold air had rushed her and the corridor outside her room wasn't there, instead she had found herself outside in the dark like she had two nights ago.

Meg had seemingly been waiting for her by the light of her torch. " Come on, I'll tell you what it is on the way. "

"Where are we going?" Emma managed to say at last, once she'd recovered from the shock of not being at home (and she had forgotten that she really needed a wee).

"Well, I was going to go and see Rain to see how he knew about Cloud, and to see if it was really true. But I got caught in an air raid and by the time that was all over and I'd come over to freshen up I had another message from Snow to go and see him" She paused for breath then continued, "the note he sent said to meet him just outside the park gates and that he had some information".

"Have you told Snow about the note Rain gave you?" asked Emma as she walked quickly beside Meg.

"Yes, he knows, and he knows what we think it means too, we'll just have to see what this other information is that he has." Meg came to an abrupt halt. "Here we are".

Emma found it hard to see exactly where they were, but they had stopped outside a set of iron gates.

It was quite a mild night, and Emma had noticed how really very dark it was. She looked up and could see the stars more clearly than she had ever seen them. There were no street lights on and the houses that were nearby the entrance of the park were all in complete darkness too. Where was everybody? Before Emma could ask Meg, a tall figure approached them.

"It's him" Meg said. She turned towards the man walking briskly towards them. "Snow" She said with a nod. The man was tall and dark, but Emma couldn't really see his face, he had a trilby hat on which was pulled quite low over his eyebrows.

"Meg" Snow returned her nod. "You must be Emma" he didn't say anything else to Emma, but as he glanced her way, Emma saw a flash of moustache. He turned his attention to Meg. "Of course we are all concerned about the information that Rain gave you. If it is, as you say it is, we have to move fast to stop Cloud from sending any more warnings to the Germans about Operation Neptune. We have him tailed as we speak and we have made sure he can't send any telegrams without us knowing about them. The only way he can make contact with the other side is to leave the country and attempt to cross the Channel." His voice was assured, very clear and arrogant. He was obviously used to being listened to.

Meg looked thoughtful at this speech, "What about Rain?" she said.

"Rain has disappeared since he gave you the note, we have eyes looking for him but no news yet." Snow said. He looked down as if disappointed at this failure. His hands clenched in to fists with obvious frustration.

Emma was listening to all this and just about following what was being said. She felt intimidated but remembered that Meg had mentioned a third Agent who was under suspicion. "What about Hail?" she suddenly said, surprising herself.

Both Meg and Snow turned to look at Emma as if they were just remembering she was there. "Hail is the one I wanted to talk to you about" said Snow, looking back at Meg. "He's also gone missing." Emma almost expected a "de-de-der" like in the Scooby-Doo cartoons she sometimes watched. Snow did look like a caricature of a spy in some respects, the darkness he oozed as well as the darkness he was standing in.

"But you said you had some information" said Meg. She was getting a little alarmed about the fact that two of the Agents she suspected of what can only be called treason, were unaccounted for. As Snow was about to reply, Meg's torch light went out. "Oh bother!" Meg shook the useless torch but it was well and truly dead.

"Here" said Emma, "Use this" she handed Meg her phone. It lit up Meg's surprised face with a blue glow.

47

"Err, thanks" Meg managed to say. Snow grabbed the phone out of her hands.

"What the hell is this?" he said loudly. He peered at it closely and even gave it a sniff.

"It's my phone" said Emma, "I just thought it would help you to see in the dark a bit"

Snow was now holding it between his fingertips as if it was something dangerous. He dared to hold it a little tighter and brought it back closer to his face. He looked like he was going to ask something but Meg interrupted.

"Information? Snow? What is it?"

Snow gathered himself and handed the phone back to Meg. He cleared his throat, "This" he said and handed Meg a note.

Meg unfolded the note and used the light from Emma's phone to read what it said.

" Graupel? " She read. "Where did you get this?"

Snow rubbed his hand across his forehead. "I don't know" he said, "it just appeared on my desk at HQ". His eyes flickered up at Emma, she could see the almost navy blue of them as they flashed in the phone light.

Meg looked at the note again. "Graupel? Is that German?"

"It might be "said Snow, "It sounds like it but I've no idea what it means, I thought you might know, I haven't shown it to our interpreters yet"

Emma glanced at Meg, "Why would someone who was a German spy write a message in German?" She said.

No one really knew what to say. Each were lost in their own thoughts and theories. Suddenly, an engine roared into life. The car it belonged to appeared out of the shadows and screeched past them. It's headlights were barely visible, pointing down to the ground, and there was no way of knowing the registration or even the make of the car.

"Get down!" shouted Snow, he grabbed Emma's glowing phone and threw it away, presumably so whoever was in the car wouldn't see their faces. It was a bit late for that, the noise of the car had faded and all that was left was a faint smell of exhaust.

"Who was that?" Emma asked, shrugging off Snow's grip, he had grabbed her and Meg and dragged them to the ground.

"Get off me" she said as she struggled to her feet, Emma gingerly crossed the road in search of her phone.

Meg and Snow got to their feet. "Who do you think that was?" Meg said, brushing the dirt from her dress.

"I don't know" said Snow, "Let's hope whoever it was wasn't close enough to hear what we were saying" He clenched one fist again and pounded it into his other hand.

As they waited for Emma to return from the darkness both Snow and Meg were having similar thoughts. The car probably belonged to one of the missing Agents, but which one? After a few minutes Meg shouted out into the darkness. Emma wasn't coming back, she had disappeared.

Emma was disappointed to find herself back in her room. At least she had found her phone before she came back. She was far too excited to go back to bed. She glanced at the screen, 'missed call' – it was from Lea. Probably nothing important, Emma thought, probably about homework, Lea always left it until the last moment.

Emma had done all of hers, of course, but she got her lap top out to do a bit of extra work now. She wanted to type in the new message that Snow had given Meg earlier. She looked up the definition of "graupel". She read "The main forms of precipitation include drizzle, rain, sleet, snow, graupel and hail." But what was graupel? Apparently "soft hail or snow pellets, the word comes from the German language".

Emma sat back and looked away from the screen. This was all too confusing. Who had written the note? Rain or Cloud? Were they trying to say something about Hail? Why had those words been written in German? If it was Rain then what was all that stuff about Cloud? Was it all rubbish? But what if Cloud had sent the note because he knew Rain was onto him? And where was Hail in all this? The note had said a German word that can also be used in the English language. Was Hail working for both sides? Was he the double crossing agent? He had disappeared, according to Snow. They had to find him to be able to decipher any of this.

Emma's head began to ache and her eyes were sore, she would have to try and get some sleep. And there was school in the morning.

Meg had left Snow shortly after Emma had gone and made her way slowly back to her flat. It was difficult without her torch to guide her but she had made it all the way back to her front door when she fell over something and landed in a heap on the ground. "Blast it!" she said into the darkness.

She struggled to her feet when she heard a match being struck and a face light up in its glare. "Hail!" Meg said as she straightened herself up. "Where did you spring from?"

Hail slowly blew out the smoke from his cigarette. "I've been waiting for you" he said. "You been somewhere nice?"

Meg tried to read his expression but it was far too dark. Had he been the mystery car driver? "Why don't you come in and we can talk" She unlocked the door and led him up the communal stairs. Miss Higgins, the landlady, strictly forbid any male visitors into her lodgings so Meg put her fingers to her lips as she motioned for Hail to go inside.

The hallway smelt of damp and the flowery wallpaper was peeling off quite alarmingly. As they climbed the stairs Meg missed out the third from top one that always creaked and pointed at it so Hail would do the same.

Meg fumbled with her key and let them both in to her pokey flat. It was tiny really and pretty empty. The living area was made up of a sofa, moulting horsehair from various holes, a table, which Meg had optimistically put a bright, red, gingham cloth over to cheer the place up a bit and a small stove, piled high with pots, pans and mugs.

When they were settled at Meg's cheery table with an obligatory calming cup of tea each, Hail began to explain where he had been and what he knew. He still had a strong German accent but his English was pretty flawless.

"I've been tailing Rain since I heard that someone was sending messages back to Germany about the Operation and I thought I was getting close to finding some answers" He took a noisy gulp from his tea," I found out that Rain sent a telegram last week to an address in Dover."

Meg made a motion to interrupt but Hail waved his hand and continued "It turned out to be a red herring, nothing, just a note to a prisoner of war there - his brother- they regularly write and there was nothing untoward about it as far as I (or the censors) could see".

Hail took another loud slurp of tea, "Then I heard that Rain had sent you a note". He waited to see if Meg would confirm or deny this. When she did neither, he continued. "Did he say that Cloud was the traitor?"

Again Meg didn't say anything.

"Well, if he did, I can tell you that he's got it wrong, Cloud would never turn back. Since being trained by MI5 he's 100% loyal to King and country, I'd bet my life on it" Hail sat back on his chair with his arms outspread as if to physically show that he was being honest. "My money is still on Rain, and I think if I have a bit more time, I can prove it."

Meg really didn't know what to make of Hail's little outburst. Her instinct was not to trust him, but there was no concrete reason as to why she should feel like this. They had worked together for nearly two years and successfully captured many enemy spies. There was just something that was nagging at her. What was it? Why didn't she believe him? Hail was very weasel –like in the way he looked, with small eyes and a sharp pointy nose, Meg had never been one to judge someone on their looks alone. But his whiskery moustache certainly didn't help endear him to her either.

Suddenly there was a loud crashing noise and it sounded as if another bomb had gone off. Meg ran to the window to look out. She was just in time to catch a glimpse of a man, who had evidently just broken down the front door below and was disappearing into her communal hallway.

She didn't have much time to escape. She shouted at Hail to standby and took her gun from her bag. Hail took his gun out too and they both waited.

It seemed like an age before there was a sound outside Meg's door. She heard a man's voice shout "Get back inside". Miss Higgins had obviously heard her front door being destroyed and poked her head out to see what the commotion was. Meg was aware of Miss Higgins giving a little shriek of alarm. But Meg was already lowering her gun. She had recognised the voice.

Instead, Meg turned round to Hail and pointed her gun at him.

"What the hell are you doing?" Hail said in a loud whisper through clenched teeth, "There's a man outside about to burst in here and you're pointing your gun at ME?"

Snow burst into the room and trained his gun on Hail too. "Stay where you are" He said. "Meg? Are you alright?" he allowed a quick sideways glance at Meg but his attention was mainly on Hail, who still hadn't lowered his own gun yet. "Put the gun down" Snow said firmly.

"What is this?" Hail said. "I came here to talk to Meg, that's all, you can't possibly think it's me that's the traitor?" Hail looked genuinely hurt but Snow kept his gun pointing at his head.

"I said put the gun down" Snow said again. Hail had no choice with two guns pointing at him, he put down the gun and kicked it across to Snow. He raised his hands up but continued to protest his innocence.

"Look, you've got it wrong. I've just been telling Meg I think I'm onto Rain, it's him you should be after, not me."

"You can explain it all to me back at HQ" Snow said as he motioned with his gun for Hail to start walking towards the door. "I really do want to hear what you've got to say, but you have to understand that if I see one of my agents waiting outside another agent's house in the middle of the night I have to act swiftly and with suspicion" There was that arrogant tone again, he was so sure of what he was saying.

Snow and Hail had reached the communal hallway. Snow spoke over his shoulder to Meg who had followed them down the stairs. "You go back inside, I'll take it from here. See if you can find out where Rain has disappeared too. At least we know where Cloud and this one is now" he nodded towards Hail as he spoke.

Meg tried to close the broken door as best she could and lent the hat stand across it before going back upstairs to her room. Now she really was confused. She decided not to think about who may have

52

done what and try to settle down. Her heart was still racing and she realised that she still had her gun in her hand.

She suspected that her landlady was peering out from a crack in a door somewhere but she wasn't in the mood for questions. She would have to get some rest before morning, she had another ambulance shift starting at 7 and she had to figure out where to start looking for Rain as soon as she could.

Chapter Nine

After a restful Sunday and a disappointingly quiet Sunday night, free from any drama, Emma was surprisingly alert at school the following day. She hadn't had much sleep at all over the past two nights but she was still buzzing from what she'd been through with Meg, but she had been for a run on Sunday afternoon and cleared her head. Running for Emma was such a release, she always felt so free. She hadn't ever stopped to think why she loved it so much. Her mum always joked that she was running away from her real life – well, her real life was so messed up at the moment, maybe Diana was right.

"Emma, could I please borrow your ruler?" Lucy was sitting next to Emma in Maths as she usually did, and, as she usually did, she was asking to borrow Emma's equipment. What kind of person comes to school with no pencil case? Lucy never had a ruler with her, or a pencil, or even a pen to write with. Emma sighed and handed over her ruler. She was a patient girl but she was getting a little tired of lending, then inevitably losing, her stuff to Lucy. The maths room was stuffy and smelt of stale sweat. The lesson before lunch was always hard, everyone was so hungry and, although not looking forward to actually eating the school dinners on offer, everyone was in desperate need of something to pick them up.

Miss Ross was waffling on in the background about fractions or something and the form were all looking confused and muttering to each other. It wasn't the most focused of classes and Emma glanced more than once at the clock on the wall. Time seemed to have stood still. But Emma didn't want to think too deeply about the matter of time. If she started to think what time was and where and when she had been recently, her brain really might explode. She could see Lucy looking over at her exercise book and blatantly copying, but Emma wasn't entirely sure it was right anyway so didn't mind too much.

At last the bell rang for lunch. There was an audible sigh of relief from everyone. Emma noticed Lucy slipping her ruler into her own bag but she didn't say anything. She walked out to the playground and met up with Lea, Sarah and Zoe. Lucy disappeared off somewhere else.

The playground was full of groups huddled together chatting and eating. Emma missed primary school where breaks were called play time and she actually got to play games and run about rather than just stand still and get cold. Lea was chatting away between mouthfuls of crisps. "So, I said to her, I said sorry Miss, but I really don't understand this and she said, well, Lea, if you spent more time listening to me when I explain things and less time talking to your friends maybe you would understand it, and then she didn't even help me, I was well cross" Emma tuned around and spotted Lucy walking towards the school gates.

"Hey, where's Lucy going?" she said, interrupting Lea's indignant speech.

They all turned to watch Lucy crossing the playground. She pressed the button to speak to reception, there was a faint buzz and the school gates opened. Lucy walked straight out of school. She had her head bowed slightly and her feet were hardly leaving the ground as she slunk out.

"She shouldn't be leaving school at lunch time" said Lea, with relish, sensing another drama, "she's so odd".

"Don't be horrible, Lea" said Emma, sharply. She surprised herself at her tone but she really was getting annoyed at Lea, who always seemed to have something to say about everything – and usually not very nice things – she was turning in to such a gossip.

"I was just saying" said Lea, "I don't see you being nice to Lucy very often either you know". Emma thought that was another mean thing to say, but she didn't say so. She promised herself that she'd try to be nicer to Lucy.

"Maybe I'll pop round to see her on my way home tonight" Emma said. She knew where Lucy lived, although she'd never been there. But as soon as the words left her mouth, she regretted them. Now Lea would turn her mean-ness on Emma.

"Maybe you should" said Lea as she linked arms with Zoe and walked off. Emma was used to Lea's moods but it was so hard work being her friend sometimes. She used to just shut up and not say anything when Lea started saying things she didn't agree with, but

55

recently she couldn't stop herself challenging Lea. Emma knew that her position as Lea's best friend was in jeopardy but found that she wasn't all that bothered.

The afternoon went by quite quickly at school. It was PE, Emma's favourite. She enjoyed the mindless running around and worked up quite a sweat during dodgeball. She had been on the winning team but had taken quite a few blows to the body from the ball when she hadn't managed to swerve in time. The opposition's best player? Lea, of course. She had hurled that ball with such power it was a wonder that no-one hurt themselves.

It was only when she was changed back into her school uniform and brushing her hair that Emma remembered what she'd said to Lea. She really didn't want to go round to Lucy's house but now she'd said it out loud she didn't feel like she could back out now.

As she grabbed her bag off her peg, Lea called after her, "Say hello to Lucy for me!" Emma said nothing as the bell went and it was time to go.

Lucy's house was only slightly out of the way for Emma, and she knew her mum wouldn't notice if she was a bit late back. Her mum was probably not even home anyway, she was still spending most afternoons at the hospital with great Nan, despite the signs that she was getting better.

Emma approached an end of terrace house with a huge skip of rubbish just outside it. Emma stood outside Lucy's front door and hesitated. She could hear the sound of the television from the inside – some sort of daytime chat show with audience laughter and applause erupting every now and then. The street was quite empty, she could leave now and Lea wouldn't know she hadn't gone round. But Emma felt defiant. Lea had been so horrible to Lucy, and besides, Emma was naturally curious (nosey!), she wanted to know why Lucy had left school early.

Emma rang the bell and bit her nails as she waited. The sound of the television stopped abruptly but no one came to answer the door. Emma rang the bell again, maybe Lucy hadn't heard it over the sound of her programme. Lucy's voice broke the silence from inside, "Who is it?" she said.

"It's me, Emma" said Emma through the door, "I was just on my way home and wanted to see if you were alright".

"I'm alright" the voice came from inside, "Just didn't feel well so I came home early".

"Oh" said Emma. Were they going to have a whole conversation through the door or was she going to be asked inside? There was a little sound of movement from inside, but Lucy didn't say anything else. She certainly didn't invite Emma in.

"OK then" said Emma, "As long as you're alright"

She made to leave when Lucy spoke again. "I would invite you in but the place is a mess and my mum doesn't really want anyone seeing it like this, sorry". It was a gabble of words spoken so fast that Emma could barely catch it.

"OK then" Emma said again. "Bye". She walked back down Lucy's path and turned back for home. She looked back at the house as she left and saw a tiny movement of the curtain at the window. Emma knew that something wasn't quite right but she had too many other dramas going on to think about another one – Meg would surely come again tonight and she needed to tell her about "graupel", plus her mum would be home very soon and want to tell her all about how Nan was doing. She'd probably want her to visit her at the hospital again too. No, Lucy and whatever was going on with her, would have to wait for another day. Emma hurried off down the road, home to her mum.

Lucy's mum, Laura, was not really like any of Lucy's friends' mums. She was still quite young for a start, she had Lucy when she was seventeen – the pregnancy was a mistake, of course, and one that Laura liked to remind Lucy of at least twice a day. Lucy's dad, Mark, had cleared off pretty sharpish, unfortunately, and it had been just the two of them ever since. Laura was also very loud. A fact that was amplified, quite literally, in the confines of such a small house.

She was also never home until Lucy had gone to bed and Lucy often found herself on her own all evening. To be fair, Laura was doing her best. Lucy always had a sandwich waiting for her when she got home from school, usually with a post-it note stuck to it saying something about how much she was loved. But what Lucy wanted more than anything was for her mum to be there to tell her all those things in person. Actually, what she wanted more than anything in the world at that very moment was another sandwich filling- cheese for what felt like the fiftieth time that week was not helping Lucy's bad mood. Lucy sat back on her sofa in her empty house and put the television back on. What else was there to do?

Chapter Ten

Meg was racking her brains. Where would Rain go? How could he just disappear? He must've been the one to put the note on Snow's desk yesterday, but no one had seen him do it and no one had seen him since. She was just parking up the ambulance after another gruelling shift. Florrie had been particularly chatty after finding out her American soldier wasn't quite as wonderful as she thought he was. Meg would be glad to get home and, hopefully, meet Emma. Two brains were better than one, Meg needed all the help she could get.

"Bye Florrie!" she called out as she left the ambulance station, but Florrie was already walking towards a man in a GI uniform who had been waiting for them as they'd driven in. Maybe Florrie was ready to overlook any shortcomings and give him another chance.

It was already quite dark when Meg let herself in. She'd just got upstairs when she heard a noise from inside her flat. Not again, she thought, had Snow come back to give her more information? Or was it Hail again? Had he been cleared of suspicion already? Meg got her gun out of her bag, just in case, and crept towards her door. She braced herself and took a deep breath. "3,2 1 " she muttered under her breath before she burst in through her door and swung her gun around.

Emma froze as the door burst open and Meg ran in with her gun pointing every which way. "It's me! It's only me!" she yelled in a shaky voice.

Meg lowered her gun and looked relieved as she saw who it was. "Don't do that!" she said, "I could've killed you".

Emma hadn't really thought about the danger of the situation she found herself in. She had just been concentrating on the strange messages and who the bad guy was, not the fact that the bad guy could be a potential killer of Meg, of her, of whoever was in his way.

Meg sat down heavily on a chair at the table and Emma joined her. Emma was still in her school uniform. She hadn't even got to her bedroom, just inside the house when she found herself in a different place altogether. She was proud of herself for deducing (look at that! 'A spy word'!) it was Meg's flat she was in – there were stockings drying over the chair and a red lipstick on the table.

"So," Meg said, she had her ambulance uniform on, a sort of green jumpsuit, the same outfit she had worn when she had visited Emma's room four nights ago. "What are your thoughts about this latest note? Did you find out what graupel is?"

Emma explained to her that it meant hail and it was a word that could be used in the English or the German language. Meg looked thoughtful, "So it could mean that Hail is being used by the English and the Germans too? He's the double crosser?"

"That's what I thought" said Emma, "But who sent the note? Can you trust the note to be true or is it just trying to throw you off course? I thought Cloud was the one you suspected after that first note".

Meg put her head in her hands. "I'm so confused".

She told Emma about her encounter with Hail. Emma's eyes widened at the part about Snow bursting in and the nearly - gun - battle "I think it's safe to say that Miss Higgins is not happy with me and I expect a bill for a new front door very soon." Meg gave a little smile.

It was very exciting but becoming too real. Someone could get really hurt. It was Emma's turn to put her head in her hands. "We have to find Rain" she said.

Meg nodded. "Let's get some fresh air" she said, rising from her chair. "Come on, I'll get us some tea at Lyons".

Meg locked the door behind them as they walked out into the warm, darkening night. "By the way" she said, "Let's have a look at your phone again, I couldn't believe it when you showed me that last night"

Emma handed her the phone. "Just look at it!" Meg went on, "It's amazing! And it plays music? And you can make calls?"

Emma was about to answer when a loud siren started wailing.

"Blast it!" Meg said, "Air raid. Come on"

She took Emma's hand and led her to a public shelter. Lots of people were making their way there. It was still quite early in the evening. Some people were dressed in their work clothes, some had

60

already dressed up for a night out. Some people were half way between the two, with hair in rollers or dressing gowns over their outfits that weren't quite on yet.

The siren noise got a little quieter as Emma and Meg descended the stairs further down into the shelter. Emma was amazed at how many people were milling around down there. Meg got them both a cup of tea, not quite what she had in mind when they'd stepped out of her flat earlier, but tea all the same.

"Let's find somewhere to sit down" Meg said, "We could be here for a while".

Emma jumped as she heard the bangs from outside. She had a feeling that they were bombs but she didn't want to think that thought too hard.

"Don't worry, we're quite safe down here" Meg said as another bomb went off and vibrated through the whole place. "At least, we have been so far" she said a little quieter.

Emma looked around. "Just keep your eyes open" she muttered to herself. She saw lots of suspicious looking people, but, really they were probably just scared people. Emma had got far too into her role as the partner of a spy, she trusted no one.

"So tell me a bit more about yourself" Meg said, "We really don't know each other that well, do we?" Emma thought of what she could say that wouldn't sound boring. "Well, I'm in year 8 at school and I like athletics and reading and hanging out with my friends and…" another bomb hit far up above them, "and I live with my brother and my mum and dad, and my great Nan, we have a cat too and…" she paused, she did sound boring, she thought, "but Nan is ill in hospital at the moment, she seems to be getting better, she's really old, but all there" Emma tapped the side of her head with her finger. "And that's it really".

Meg smiled, "what are your friends like?" she asked.

"Erm" said Emma, "really nice most of the time, there's Lea, my best friend I suppose, although we've sort of fallen out at the moment, then there's Sarah and Zoe, and, well, Lucy" Emma wasn't sure if Lucy technically counted as a friend but she was still feeling guilty about not going into her house earlier to make sure she was ok, so she thought she'd include her.

Emma waited for Meg to ask another question but Meg seemed to be looking just beyond Emma's shoulder at something behind her. Emma turned round to see what or who it was but she didn't really know what she was looking for. Meg turned back to Emma and smiled even more brightly than before. "I thought I just saw Cloud" she said through her gritted smiling teeth.

"Cloud?" said Emma, a little too loudly, and then quieter, "But Snow said he was being watched, didn't he?"

"It doesn't mean he knows he's being watched" said Meg. She tried to look around again but there were so many people in the shelter that whoever it was she saw had disappeared into the throng. The bombs were falling thick and fast now, Emma was getting a little nervous that the roof wouldn't hold. She knew that she was many metres underground but the noise was still quite loud and the vibrations were felt throughout her body. Plus, she didn't know how she was going to get home. What if she couldn't? She'd promised mum that she would visit Nan with her tomorrow after school.

"There he is!" Meg said, breaking into Emma's thoughts. "He's coming over". A tall man in a grey suit, wearing a bowler hat and carrying an umbrella walked towards them.

"I know he's supposed to look English, but that's a bit much, isn't it?" Emma said in a loud whisper.

Meg giggled, then composed herself. "Hello there" she said to the man as he reached them.

Cloud glanced at Emma, "Fancy seeing you here" he said, flashing a rather fetching smile. He was very handsome, she could see that now. A thick mop of dirty blonde hair and a square jaw, dusted with stubble. Emma even felt herself blush as he turned in her direction and held out his hand. "Pleased to meet you...?"

"Emma" Emma said, filling in his hanging question.

"Emma" he repeated, "Would you mind awfully if I borrowed Meg for a quick chat, won't be long"

"Don't worry" said Meg, "Whatever you have to say you can say in front of Emma," she lowered her voice "She knows everything".

Cloud looked a bit startled, but soon regained his cool, just as another explosion made a loud noise above. "I hope your flat's still standing after all this" he said, with an inappropriate smile. Emma decided the smile was not so dashing after all, it had a bit of a sneer about it.

"What is it, Cloud?" Meg said, impatiently. She had almost made up her mind that he was not the one they were looking for and she was getting a little tired of the time wasting.

"I thought you'd like to know where our friend, Rain was, that's all" Cloud said, a bit too casually. Meg and Emma exchanged glances.

"Out with it then," Meg said.

"He's got a brother, apparently, in Dover" Cloud said with a shrug. "Prisoner of war." He paused, "I suppose that could've been Rain in there too if you hadn't turned him." He looked Meg directly in the eyes, "Or me, I suppose" he said quietly.

"We know about his brother" Meg said, "He writes to him. The censors give us copies of the letters so we know what he says. Nothing very exciting most of the time as far as we can tell"

"Well, that's where we might have dropped the ball, you see," Cloud said, "Rain said he wants to visit his brother."

"The authorities would never allow it" Emma said, she didn't know how she knew this but it seemed pretty obvious.

"You're right" Cloud said, "But I know for a fact that he is getting on a train to Dover on Thursday, leaving from St Pancras at 7 o' clock that evening"

"To visit his brother?" Meg said with a note of disbelief. "I don't buy that, Cloud, he wouldn't be that blatant in disobeying orders. Besides, how do you know all this? How do we know it's not nonsense?"

"Well, you don't do you?" he said as another bomb, the loudest of the night, exploded closely overhead. "You'll just have to take my word for it like Snow did".

"You've been talking to Snow?" Meg said. She thought about the first note again. Had Cloud been talking to someone higher up to climb higher up the ranks? Was Snow the man higher up?

As Cloud, Emma and Meg stood lost in their own thoughts, the noise of the bombing seemed to have stopped. There was still a lot of noise inside the station, chatting and a bit of laughing, but the vibrations from the explosions had definitely stopped.

63

"I'm just telling you what I know" Cloud said, "You can choose to ignore me if you want but I'm just saying that Rain will be at St Pancras on Thursday night. Whether he's going to visit his brother, try to get a message to Germany or visiting the white cliffs, I don't know, but there you are" He held out his hands, palms up, then he walked away.

The sirens for the all clear signalled and everyone started to gather anything they'd brought with them and make a move for the stairs.

"Thank goodness that didn't last as long as they usually do, we could've been in here all night. Come on, we'll go back to mine, we have a lot to talk about". Meg and Emma got jostled along as they made their way upwards. Cloud had disappeared already and as the crowds pushed and shoved, Emma found herself losing sight of Meg too.

She managed to get out into the night air but Meg was nowhere to be seen. What she did see was fire. Fire everywhere. Burning buildings and huge jets of water from the fire engines, that didn't seem to be making much headway. The smell of burning was unbearable, and the heat, even though Emma was a fair distance away, she could feel the warmth of the flames licking at her face. Some people were walking towards the fires, the unlucky ones, Emma thought, whose homes once stood there, some people had turned away, to keep calm and carry on.

Emma waited where she was to see if Meg would reappear. When it became apparent that she wouldn't, Emma decided to walk back towards the direction of Meg's flat. The fires lit up the street so she thought she knew the way, but as she approached Meg's damaged front door she found it was unlocked. She opened it and walked through, finding herself back in her own bedroom.

Chapter Eleven

"Emma! That's the third time I've called you! Get up!" Diana called up the stairs. Emma groaned and swung her legs out of bed. Surely she'd only just got into bed. It couldn't be morning time already? "Coming!" She shouted back.

As she was brushing her teeth her head cleared a bit and she remembered about the fires and what Cloud had said. As she spat into the sink she thought of those families who found themselves homeless and possession-less. She vowed to be thankful for what she had. She also vowed to be nicer to Lucy, she had seemed even more weird than usual yesterday. Emma decided to keep her spy hat on and find out what was going on there. Besides, she thought, Lea was probably still cross with her for yesterday so she would have lots of chances to talk to Lucy alone.

"Don't forget to come straight home after school today –you hadn't forgotten about visiting Nan had you? Diana said as she passed Emma the milk for her Cheerios.

"No, of course not" Emma lied. She really didn't want to sit beside Nan again and hear her weird ramblings, she felt guilty for feeling like that, Nan was in her nineties after all, how amazing was that? And she had said some things last time which Emma may need to clarify. She really was beginning to think like a spy. She quickly ate her cereal and grabbed a piece of toast on her way out.

Lea wasn't waiting for Emma as she usually was, outside the form room. Emma walked in and found Lea, Zoe and Sarah huddled in one corner and Lucy sitting on her own in another. Emma looked at both options and hesitated. Whichever one she chose would feel like a betrayal so she took a deep breath and walked casually over to Lucy.

Lucy had her headphones in and had not heard Emma approaching, which made it even more awkward. Emma stood next to her and shifted her weight from one foot to the other, waiting for Lucy to notice her. She gave a little cough and looked over at Lea's little gang who were laughing loudly. She was just about to grab a book from near Lucy and pretend that was why she'd gone over there as she returned to Lea, when Lucy tugged out her earphones and said hello.

"Oh hi Lucy" Emma said, "You feeling better?" Lucy looked a little blank. Then she seemed to remember her excuse for leaving school yesterday. "Er, yes thanks, much better" she said.

There was an uncomfortable silence developing. "What are you listening to?" Emma said quickly. She'd always hated small talk but she really couldn't think of anything else to say. "Oh, just the new one from Devil's Watch." said Lucy.

"I don't think I've heard that" said Emma, "Can I have a listen?" Lucy reluctantly handed Emma an earphone. Emma shoved it into her ear and heard the loudest racket she had ever heard. It was a mixture of very very loud guitar with a throbbing drum beat and a screeching vocal. She quickly took it out again and said "wow! That's er, very loud" She looked at Lucy who's face had changed somewhat. No longer was she looking fearful and nervous, she was trying to supress a laugh.

She couldn't hold it in, Lucy burst out laughing, "You could say that!"

Emma laughed too, "Oh my goodness! It's awful!" she said through her giggles.

"It takes a few listens to get used to" Lucy said, she was still smiling. Emma felt a new feeling of warmth towards Lucy. She was so hard to get through to but when she opened up and had a laugh she seemed like such a lovely person.

"Here" said Emma, offering Lucy her own earphones, "Listen to some real music for a change" and she found her favourite song on her phone for Lucy to listen to - the one she used for her ringtone by Darkness Rises.

Lucy and Emma had a nice day at school together. They even stood with Lea, Sarah and Zoe at lunch break, but Lucy and Emma were still talking about music so didn't really speak to them much. At last the final bell went. Lucy slipped the ruler she had taken yesterday back into Emma's bag and started to walk towards the school gates. Emma ran to catch up with her.

"Would you like to come back to my house sometime after school this week? Say, tomorrow?" she said when she was walking beside her.

Lucy had closed up again, Emma could tell. She was stuttering over her words and was looking a little bit nervous again. Emma was confused. Surely they'd just had a really nice day together.

"I'll have to see what my mum says" Lucy finally managed to say, "Bye". And she walked briskly away.

Emma walked briskly too. She had promised not to dawdle so they could get to the hospital before the rush hour began. As she walked she allowed herself to think about what might happen after the hospital visit, when she hopefully saw Meg again. Meg had warned her that she might not be able to see her tonight. She had to find Rain before Wednesday night, just in case Cloud had been telling the truth and Rain was getting on that Dover train. Emma hoped she would find herself helping Meg, but she really didn't know how all this time travelling worked (time travelling? Emma giggled to herself! When she thought it 'out loud' like that it sounded highly implausible!). She rushed through the front door to find an empty house.

"Mum?" she called out. She walked back outside and noticed that the car was not in the drive. "Mum?" She said again, a bit more quietly this time. She knew her mum wasn't there. She noticed a note on the kitchen table, propped up behind the ketchup bottle. It was from her mum, telling her that she was at the hospital. Emma's Nan had suddenly taken a turn for the worse.

Emma dialled her mum's mobile phone and heard it ring upstairs. What was the point of having a mobile phone if you never took it with you? Emma didn't know what to do with herself. To break into her thoughts, Owen burst through the door. "Where's mum?" he said, heading straight for the bread bin. He shoved two pieces of bread in the toaster and proceeded to get out butter, marmite, jam, cheese and whatever else he could find for his usual after school snack.

"She's at the hospital" Emma said, handing him the note. Even Owen had the sensitivity to stop buttering his toast as he digested the news. "Oh poor mum" he said. Emma and Owen both loved their

Nan, of course, but they could see that it was their mum who had been suffering these past few weeks. Nan was old. She was bound to go sooner rather than later. Emma was just very sad for her mum who had to get her head round losing her ma, then being told she was on the mend, and now to this again.

"I'm off upstairs to do my homework" Emma said as she grabbed a piece of Owen's toast. Owen's protests followed her upstairs to her room. She sat down heavily on the bed and half heartedly got her books out. Dad wouldn't be home until late and she would be expected to get some sort of tea together for Owen and herself. Sometimes being the eldest, and a girl, was a real pain.

She decided that she really wasn't in the mood to do any homework so she put on some music instead. She started to sing and before too long she had forgotten all about her Nan and her mum and anything else that was going on in her head. She belted out a few other songs before getting out her laptop and looking for some other songs to download. Strangely, she found herself looking up Devils Watch. She chose three songs to put onto her phone. "The Call of Duty", "Kick me, I'm hurting" and "Guns can kill". They sounded all pretty much the same. Very loud and full of drums but Emma found that Lucy had been right. The more she listened to them the more she liked them.

She was just listening to "Guns can kill" for the fourth time when she heard Owen calling her name. Inexplicably, he was hungry again. She'd have to go downstairs and sort her useless brother out.

Emma's dad drove Emma and Owen to the hospital that evening. They found Diana leaning on Nan's bed, gently snoring. Richard walked over to her and gently stroked her cheek to wake her up. "Oh hello" She managed to say, "No change, I'm afraid".

Emma looked over at Nan lying in the bed. She looked quite grey but she was breathing. "Is there any point us actually being here?" Owen said, looking fed up.

"Owen!" Richard said sharply, "Don't be so horrid". He glanced over at mum, but Diana looked so tired that she probably hadn't heard Owen's comment anyway.

Emma glanced around the ward. It was full of grey looking old ladies and people talking in hushed tones. There were a few nurses efficiently walking around, some with clipboards, some helping some of the old ladies to walk around. The smell of illness was in the air, not even the disinfectant could disguise it. There was also an underlying smell of something else. Emma couldn't quite put her finger on it, a sort of sweet smelling smell, quite familiar. Wee! That was it. Emma really wanted to be somewhere else.

"Is there anything to read in here?" she asked her mum.

Diana rummaged around in the bedside cupboard. "Not really" she said. She pulled out a few bits of paper and tissues. "Oh, there's this", she handed Emma a magazine. It was one of those magazines which told you what to eat, what to wear and showed celebrities with their wardrobe mistakes.

"Thanks", said Emma, flicking through the pages. She wasn't really looking at it, but as she turned to the puzzle pages at the back, she found a partially completed crossword. Emma liked word games so she had a look to see if she could finish it.

The words didn't seem to make sense. There were a couple of right answers, but then Emma found her own name. She also found the word Neptune. Was this another coded message about Meg's mission? She quickly scanned the crossword. She found Hail and she found Snow. She could feel herself getting hot and sweat prickled under her armpits. Keep your head, she thought to herself. She looked again. One down said Emma, two across – Look at, three down – third note don't, four across – listen to, five down – C Victoria. Emma paused. What was the third note? Meg hadn't found another note yet, just the first two. C must be Cloud, surely? But why was the name Victoria there? Was Nan really so confused that she'd forgotten her own great granddaughters name? She carried on, six across –behind, seven down – tvm.

"Emma?" A voice broke into her thoughts, "Emma, I said how was school?" Diana was talking.

"Sorry, mum, yes, fine" Emma said.

"No change". Diana looked confused.

"Oh, right" she said. Emma went back to looking at the crossword, tvm wasn't a word and nothing else seemed to be popping out at her, just some random words. Over, Frog, Red, Lord,

Ring, Her. Ring her? Ring Meg? How could she do that? And there was the word cloud again.

Emma tore out the crossword page from the magazine and put it in her coat pocket.

"How about a quick game?" said her dad getting out the travel scrabble.

The next half an hour was spent arguing over what words were real words and which were slang and not allowed. No-one had brought a dictionary with them so a lot of the arguments ended with huffs or stropps from Emma or Owen, (are those slang words?).

Nan didn't move or make a sound during the whole game.

"Mum, can we go home now, please", said Owen for the tenth time. Even Richard didn't tell him off for being insensitive this time, he looked at his watch and motioned to Diana that maybe it really was time to go.

"Come on, Di" he said, "They'll call us if there's any change."

Emma's mum reluctantly gathered up her things. She gave Nan a kiss on the cheek and loudly said that she'd be back in the morning. Emma and Owen dutifully kissed her too. Again, that papery skin, again that faint hint of flowery perfume, but another smell threatened to overpower it, and it wasn't a very nice smell.

"Bye Nan" Emma said, she lent over to whisper in her ear, "thank you" and she could've sworn she saw her Nan's eyelids flicker a bit.

In the car on the way home Richard started telling stories about the happier times they'd all spent with Nan. "Remember that time Emma and Owen found that massive dead crab at Woolacombe beach and scared her half to death with it?"

"Oh, I remember that" said Emma, "We called her Clawdia! Do you remember Owen?"

Owen grunted, he was plugged in to his ipod and thinking about all the television he'd missed that evening while he'd been sitting in that smelly hospital ward.

"Oh I've got one" said Diana, "Remember how she always used to put the butterscotch Angel Delight in those posh glass bowls and pretend we were having some refined dessert?"

Emma laughed. She still loved butterscotch Angel Delight, but she was thinking of another memory. It must've been about six months ago, Nan had given her a silver bangle and told her to keep it safe. She told Emma that she used to wear it when she was younger and that it had protected her from bad luck. Had she known her time was running out? Was she really going to die?

Suddenly Emma felt a huge wave of sorrow crash over her. She physically felt like a great weight had landed on her and a large lump appeared to lodge in her throat. Nan had always been there and she had taken that for granted. She honestly hadn't noticed how old and frail (and small) she had been getting. She'd always seemed so full of energy – and wit, she was so funny, and some of her jokes had not been of the cleanest kind either! She was naughty too – slipping Emma and Owen sweets behind Diana's back, allowing them to go out and play when she was babysitting rather than enforcing their normal bed time.

She had so enjoyed being their Nan, and now Emma found herself thinking about her in the past tense already.

"Try not to get upset, Em". Diana had noticed Emma's glistening eyes. "She's a fighter. She could get better still. But if she doesn't, she's had such a life".

"I know" Emma managed to say. "There's just so many things I'd like to say to her and I think I may have left it too late". She burst into tears. Diana felt her eyes well up too as the car made its way slowly home.

Chapter Twelve

Upstairs in her room Emma blew her nose and got ready for bed. It wasn't that late but crying always tired her out. She put on her dressing gown over her pyjamas and checked her phone. Three messages. As she climbed into bed to read them she actually hoped that Meg wouldn't come tonight. She still felt sad and a jumble of things and, although she wanted to tell Meg to expect a third message, she didn't think that she had anything useful to say to help the situation tonight.

Two of the messages were from Lea – the first, had Emma done her homework on the Reformation yet and the second, well? Had she? Emma felt herself liking Lea less and less. She could be so insensitive at times. Nothing in her messages asked how Emma was or how her Nan was, she was so self centred. The third message was from Lucy, it said that she could come round after school tomorrow and thanked Emma for asking. Emma cheered up a little. She put her phone down on her bedside table and picked up her book. Just a couple of chapters before lights out.

Meg's voice woke Emma up with a start. Her book fell off the bed with a thump and Emma wiped the dribble from the side of her mouth.

"Come on!" said Meg, "I've had a third message".

Emma forgot her earlier reluctance to see Meg and felt a surge of adrenaline. She was wide awake all of a sudden and ready to go. She jumped out of bed, "I got a message too" she said as she put on her slippers, "from my Nan"

"Your Nan?" said Meg in surprise. "Well, you can tell me when we get there, we've got to hurry, I never know if I'm going to get stuck here so I like to get in, get you and go, if you don't mind."

Meg was always so polite, even when she was a bit panicked. They walked out of the bedroom onto the landing, but, as was not surprising any more, instead of the landing they found themselves out in the street. Emma was surprised to find it daylight, whenever she'd been before it had been evening and getting dark, or dark already. "Where are we?" she asked.

"We're in St James' park" said Meg, "look over there and you can see Buckingham Palace".

Emma looked in the direction Meg was pointing and saw the grand house between the trees. They were walking round the lake and there were plenty of people about enjoying the sunshine. Some had ice creams and some were holding hands with men in uniform. But it looked as far away from war as Emma could imagine. Everything was so calm. "Come and sit down here with me" said Meg, "I'll tell you my message first then you can fill me in on your Nan's".

They found a couple of deckchairs and paid the attendant. "Here" said Meg, handing Emma a piece of paper.

"Fortitude at risk, don't let the weather delay you", she read. "Why do they have to write in riddles?" Emma said, although she knew really, careless talk costs lives, after all.

"Well, Operation Fortitude I do know about" said Meg, "It's our deception plan. We are feeding information to the Germans, telling them they can expect an invasion from the Allies much further East at the Pas de Calais, rather than at Normandy where the real invasion will be"

"And it's your ex German spies who are telling the Germans this?" said Emma

"Of course," said Meg, "Hail, Rain and Cloud are all part of the plan. The Germans don't' know that we've turned them. Well, we thought we'd turned them, obviously not completely as we can see from all this mess. But which one is fooling us?"

"Don't let the weather delay you" Emma read again. "Does that mean real bad weather or the Agent who has turned bad?"

"I think we can assume it's another warning about the Agent who is jeopardising the whole of Operation Neptune." said Meg.

"But no clue about which Agent really." said Emma, "would hail, cloud or rain delay a Channel crossing?"

Meg looked out over the park and didn't say anything for a full five minutes. Emma was just beginning to wonder if she had fallen into some sort of trance when Meg spoke again, "You know, if this Operation is a failure I really don't' see how Operation Overlord can be completed."

"Overlord?" said Emma, "That rings a bell"

"It's the Allied invasion of German occupied Europe." Meg said. She was just about to speak again when Emma remembered why the phrase was familiar to her. She pulled out the crossword puzzle she'd ripped from her Nan's magazine.

"Look" she said as she thrust it into Meg's face. "Over and Lord have both been written in. I thought they were just random words but they're obviously not".

Meg took the crossword and looked at all the other words that were written in. She muttered some out loud as she tried to make sense of them. "Who's Victoria?" she asked, without looking up.

"I really don't know" said Emma, "Nan's in her nineties now so she may be confused."

"Red? Ring her? This is hopeless" said Meg. "I understand the bit about not listening to Cloud, I had kind of made my mind up about that, but who is Victoria? Should we ring her? Has she got red hair?"

It was Emma's turn to stare out across the park. She noticed in the lake a big pelican dipping it's huge beak into the water looking for fish. She had in her mind something. But it was a something she couldn't grasp hold of. What was she missing? The pelican tried again to catch some lunch but failed. Red Ring her? Red Ring Her? Her Ring Red? Herring Red? Red Herring! That was it! "What if the message was telling us that Cloud was a red herring?" said Emma. "You know? Not relevant? Just put in to confuse us more?"

"Gosh!" said Meg, "You could jolly well be onto something there!" Meg smiled broadly with her whole red lipsticked face. "That's brilliant!" she said, "Now all we have to work out is who Victoria is. Let's walk for a bit"

They got up from their deckchairs and walked towards the direction of the Mall and the palace again. It was such a warm day, Emma could feel her hay fever threatening to make her eyes itch and her nose sneeze.

"What exactly did Cloud tell us during the air raid?" said Emma, rubbing her nose and trying to think back to the time they spent in

74

the shelter as the bombs raged overhead. It seemed like ages ago instead of only last night.

"He said that Rain was going to catch a train from St Pancras to Dover on Thursday night" said Meg. "It was strange him telling us that at all, I didn't really believe him, but I was going to check the station out on Thursday night if I hadn't found Rain before that"

"So that's the red herring. He is trying to confuse us, to lead us in the wrong direction, Cloud must be the bad guy?" said Emma, breathless with excitement. She clapped her hands at her apparent cleverness.

"Now don't go jumping to conclusions, "Meg said, "Cloud could be telling us stuff that he truly believes is true, Rain could've told him about St Pancras and knew he would pass it on, so Rain could be the bad guy, trying to make Cloud tell us red herrings!"

Emma looked a little deflated. Meg didn't really look triumphant either. And both were thinking about how Hail fitted into everything. He had said that Rain was the traitor too, but hadn't really produced any proof at all before Snow had taken him away.

"Achoo!" Emma's hay fever erupted. "Sorry, hay fever" said Emma, wiping her nose on the sleeve of her dressing gown. It was amazing how comfortable and unembarrassed she felt walking around in broad daylight in her bedtime clothes.

"Well, I have an ambulance shift starting in half an hour so we'd better get you back anyway," said Meg, "I think if we get a tube back to my place, you might be able to get back from there" She looked around to see which station was nearest, "Green Park" she muttered under her breath, "Green Park, Hyde Park, Victoria"

All of a sudden Meg stopped walking. Emma had heard her mutterings and stared at her. "Victoria!" they both said at once.

"Victoria means Victoria station!" said Meg. "Maybe that's where the traitor will leave London from"

Emma thought for a moment, "Do you think Thursday night is still relevant?" she said.

"Well, it's all we have for now" said Meg. "We'll just have to go there and wait. Let's see, it's Wednesday today, I will contact Snow after my shift tonight and tell him what we think and see if he has any other leads. Where, for goodness sake, is Rain?"

They hurried along to catch the tube and get back to Meg's.

Emma had managed to get back home through Meg's front door and Meg was just about be on time for work. It was, thankfully, a quiet shift. An unexploded bomb had been reported near Enfield and they had been waiting on standby just in case it went off before it could be dealt with. That took several hours and, luckily, the ambulance wasn't needed at all.

The next call was to move some patients from one hospital to another, so, again, nothing urgent or too bloody to deal with. Meg was still tired by the end of it though. She decided to walk straight to Snow and tell him what she knew, or thought she knew.

As she walked along, she tried to make sense in her head what she'd discovered but it was so confusing. She really wasn't paying attention to where she was going and didn't notice the man in the raincoat until he had charged into her, grabbed her elbow and steered her into a nearby alleyway.

Meg tried to let out a scream but a gloved hand clamped forcefully over her mouth.

"Don't you dare scream" said a man's voice in a heavily accented whisper. Meg's eyes widened as she tried to twist her body round to see who her attacker was.

"And don't struggle either". All the instincts in Meg's body were to fight but she realised that whoever had grabbed her was a lot stronger than she was. Struggling would just make him angry. She tried to hold her body still, but her legs were shaking.

"That's better" said the man. "You just hold still and this won't hurt a bit". Before Meg could react to those chilling words the man swapped the hand over her mouth with his other hand which was holding some sort of hanky that smelled of…

Meg woke up. She didn't know where she was. She was lying on a bed with her uniform still on. What had happened? She used her hand to raise herself up onto her elbows. Her head was pounding. She focussed her eyes as best she could and made out a dark figure sitting across the room from her.

"Who's there" she said with a croaky voice. "What do you want?"

The figure got up and walked towards her. He gradually came into focus and Meg felt a slight panic rise up inside. "Rain!" she gasped, "What are you doing here? Everyone's been looking for you".

Rain stood about a metre away from Meg and gave a little sigh. "I know" he said, "And I'm really sorry that I had to bring you here. I just didn't know what else to do, or another way of doing it." He ran his fingers through his messy hair and scratched his unshaven chin. "I need you to believe me, Meg. I need you to tell Snow that it's not me who is trying to muck up his plans." He walked towards her again. Meg flinched. It was hard to not be scared of someone who had just jumped you in an alleyway, drugged you and brought you back to a strange room.

"I'm really sorry about the whole chloroform thing" he said with a shrug, "I wanted to talk to you and I didn't want you to raise the alarm. It was the only way, I'm sorry" he said again, "But, please, you have to believe me." A faint thundering noise could be heard from somewhere nearby. It made the room hum a little after the sound had died away.

"What about the messages? It was you who sent them, wasn't it?" said Meg.

"Yes" said Rain, "I was trying to warn you."

"So, you think it's Cloud who's causing all the trouble?" said Meg, trying to clear her still fuggy head and remembering what conclusions Emma and her had come to yesterday in the park. "Cirrus can change colour and is climbing higher, the first message – Cloud has changed colour, changed sides? And is climbing higher – talking to people high up? That's the bit I got confused about, but then I realised you must have meant talking to people high up in Germany. Talking to the Abwehr and telling them the real destination for Operation Neptune?"

"I knew you'd understand it" Rain said with a slight smile. "You always were the best Agent at cracking codes."

"But what was the second message all about - Graupel?" said Meg

"Graupel?" said Rain, sounding surprised, "I didn't send a note saying graupel. Why would I involve Hail? It's Cloud that I was trying to tell you about. When did you get that message?"

"I didn't" said Meg, slightly surprised, "Snow said he got it and he passed it on to me"

"That's strange" said Rain, he didn't say anything else for a few seconds, "Cloud must've sent that to Snow to try to shake him off the scent"

"Like a red herring, you mean?" said Meg.

"Red Herring?" Rain's English obviously didn't stretch to funny phrases.

"Never mind" said Meg, Emma knew what she meant, she had been right, "Cloud also said that you were planning a trip to Dover on the train from St Pancras tomorrow night"

"That's ridiculous!" said Rain loudly, "My brother is a prisoner of war there, the authorities would never let me go there"

"That's what I thought" said Meg, "But why throw in another red herring? Surely that's over egging the pudding a bit"

Rain looked blank.

"Sorry, I mean it was very risky of him to try to throw us off his course with a second deception" said Meg.

Rain sat down on the side of the bed. He looked exhausted and upset. "Did you get my second message?"

"Fortitude at risk, don't let the weather delay you" said Meg, "Yes, I did. I think I worked it out. Operation Fortitude is in danger because one of the agents is going to ruin it. It wasn't very clear which one though, to be honest. Rain, Hail or Cloud can delay a Channel crossing, you know"

"Yes, but I was hoping that you'd have eliminated me and Hail from your suspicions by the time you got it. In my opinion Cloud is the most delaying weather anyway– the aeroplanes can't see what's going on to protect the boats below. Clear skies are vital in Operation Neptune" said Rain, slightly indignantly.

Meg thought she was missing something. It all seemed a bit too tidy. Why had Rain been so forceful in getting her to listen to him? Surely another message would've been easier than kidnapping her? "So, where are we?" she asked, not unreasonably.

"An underground room, perfectly safe and soundproof" said Rain
"But, where?" Meg asked again.
"Under Victoria station"

Chapter Thirteen

Emma overslept. It felt like she'd only just got into bed when her dad was shaking her awake and telling her it was time for school. She managed to crawl out of bed and splash water on her face in the bathroom but, as she caught sight of her puffy eyes and pale complexion in the mirror, she didn't feel any more awake at all.

The walk to school perked Emma up a bit. It wasn't far but she managed to walk quite briskly and think about the day ahead. She still felt confused about her situation with Meg and the uncertain future of Operation Neptune but there was nothing she could do about it while she was at school. She had still told no one, and what would she say anyway? And who would she tell? Lea was being so annoying and Zoe and Sarah were too busy talking about Maths or Boys or other things that seemed a million miles away from where Emma was in her head at the moment. Maybe she could confide in Lucy? But she really didn't know her that well and all they'd talked about was music and what lessons they had together. Besides, Emma had a feeling that Lucy had problems of her own.

Lucy was in the form room sitting on her own as usual, with her earphones in. The tinny sound of heavy rock music could be heard by anyone who passed by her desk. "Hi Lucy" said Emma , loudly, as she walked up to her. "Alright?" Lucy looked up and gave a thumbs up but she made no move to take her earphones out. Emma hovered, before she realised that Lucy obviously wasn't in the mood to speak.

"Catch you later, then?" Emma said as casually as she could as she walked over to Lea and the others.

"Told you she was weird" Lea said as a way of greeting Emma. "I wouldn't get involved if I were you" She turned to Zoe to continue her conversation "…so I said to her, if you don't like it then you know what you can do" Zoe and Sarah laughed. Emma put her bag on the table and sat down. It was not going to be a good day, she could tell.

Lucy ignored Emma for almost the whole day. Emma didn't really know what to think – Lucy was supposed to be going home with her after school and she wasn't sure if she had forgotten or if she'd just changed her mind.

The last lesson of the day was maths.

"Alright?" said Emma, a question that she'd asked Lucy at the beginning of the day, and still not got a satisfactory answer.

Lucy sat down next to Emma and nodded. She had her earphones in again, although it wasn't allowed. She had a way of getting away with things, probably because the teachers had got so fed up with telling her off, punishing her with detentions, just for her to do it again. She still got told off for the big stuff, but wearing earphones around school was often ignored.

"Do you still want to come back to mine?" Emma said, as nonchalantly as possible. The class was settling down, getting books out and waiting for Miss Ross to begin.

"Erm, yeah" said Lucy, "If that's still ok?" She had taken out her earphones and was now threading the wire through the sleeve of her jumper so that she could hold it up to her ear when she rested her head on her hand, and Miss Ross wouldn't notice.

"Of course" said Emma. She didn't say that she was surprised because Lucy had been off with her all day. But when she thought about it, Lucy had been off with everyone, and that actually wasn't unusual. Just because they had had a couple of good chats about music and maths it didn't mean that Lucy had changed. Emma thought that she really didn't want her to come home with her now, but she couldn't really say anything.

Maths dragged on and on and when the bell rang for the end of the day there was an audible sigh of relief – not just from the pupils either. Lucy and Emma packed up their things in silence then walked to the school gates together.

Usually Emma would wait for Lea and walk down to the newsagents with her, but today she felt a bit awkward so she carried on walking.

"Don't you usually wait for Lea?" Lucy asked.

"Yea, but don't worry, she knows you're coming home with me, she won't be expecting me to wait for her." Emma said hurriedly, hoping Lea wouldn't turn up and see her with Lucy. She started walking quicker down the hill, Lucy had to jog a bit to keep up.

When they arrived at Emma's house they dumped their bags in the kitchen and Emma made them a snack. They had been chatting on the way home and as school got further away, they had relaxed and had a bit of a giggle. Emma realised that she didn't know much about Lucy at all. Lucy hadn't revealed much, she was the one who had been asking most of the questions and listening to Emma waffle on. Emma had told her a little bit about her Nan and how poorly she was, (leaving out the weird crossword stuff, of course), but Lucy hadn't said anything about her family.

"Is it just you and your parents at home then? Emma asked.

Lucy took a bite of toast so she didn't have to answer straight away. "Mmm" she mumbled, spraying a few crumbs around as she did. She took a long time to swallow and once she had, didn't elaborate further. Emma waited.

"It's just me and my mum actually. Can we listen to some music" Lucy said, drawing an abrupt end to the conversation about families.

"Ok, yeah" said Emma and they went upstairs.

"I just need a wee" said Emma, "My room's that one" she pointed to the door opposite the bathroom. Lucy went in and looked around at all the posters and cuddly toys that were scattered around Emma's bedroom. It was quite a large bedroom with a lot of stuff in it. Lucy could see books piled on the bookcase and on the desk, and a messy bed covered with clothes and toys. She touched Emma's guitar with envy and strummed it a couple of times as she perched on a corner of Emma's bed to wait.

Suddenly Lucy heard the sound of the front door opening and slamming shut again. "Emma?" came Owen's voice up the stairs. Lucy expected Emma to return the call through the bathroom door but there was just silence. "Emma?" Owen called out again.

Lucy walked out onto the landing and called down, "She's in the toilet".

Owen's head appeared at the foot of the stairs. "Oh" he said, "Ok". He seemed uninterested in who Lucy was and took this stranger's word for it that Emma was home. The noise from a television floated up the stairs.

Lucy lent her ear against the bathroom door. "Emma?" she said quietly, "You ok?" There was no reply. She knocked on the door, "Emma?" she tried the handle and found that it was one of those potentially embarrassing doors that didn't lock. She pushed open the door, and a whoosh of air hit her right in the face.

When Lucy opened her eyes she found herself in a very dark street. It smelled of the night and of smoke. Where on earth was she? Her mind whirled, trying to find some logic in the situation she found herself in. Nothing. No explanation could be found. She turned round to see if the bathroom door and landing were still there, but all she could see was more street and houses.

Lucy began to feel frightened. Her heart beat quickened and she felt sweat across her top lip. It was so dark. There were no street lights on and no lights coming from any of the houses. She could hear a faint rumbling and a few people talking somewhere but it was pretty quiet. And that smell? Sort of smoky, a bit woody, what was that?

She stood there, not knowing what to do when she heard footsteps approaching. They were walking quite quickly and getting louder and louder. Someone was coming for her. She was just about to let out the loudest scream she could muster (although she was feeling so terrified she feared that it would come out as a pathetic squeak) when she heard Emma's voice. "Oh Lucy! You're here!" Emma appeared at Lucy's side and grabbed her arm.

It took a while for Lucy to find her voice. She stared at Emma. She found it very odd that Emma didn't find it very odd that her bathroom had turned into a street! "Where are we?" Lucy managed to say at last.

"It's a very long story" said Emma. "If I can find Meg, then it will be a lot easier to explain. It's weird, she's usually the one to fetch me, but I can't find her anywhere."

That was the weird thing? thought Lucy. There was a bigger weird thing as far as she was concerned. "How did we get here?" she said.

"I'm not really sure" Emma said, "It's been happening for a few nights now. I'm never really sure when it's going to happen, but when it does, it appears that I can step through some sort of time warp thing and find myself in about 1944 I think." Emma stopped talking and realised that this was the first time that she had said out loud what had been happening. Was this what had been happening? Why hadn't she questioned it more?

"1944?" Lucy said, with disbelief.

"Well, yes" said Emma, a little doubtfully. "I'm helping Meg to find a German spy. Maybe two. She works for M15 and...." Emma stopped abruptly. She remembered the posters from her History lessons – careless talk cost lives. "Let's try and find her" she said.

"Spies?" Lucy said, a little too loudly. She seemed to only be able to speak in single words.

"Come on" said Emma, she led Lucy further down the street. The rumbling sound came again, under their feet as they walked. "The Underground" said Emma, "there must be a station nearby, let's see" They carried on walking through the darkness. More people seemed to join the direction they were heading and they very quickly came to the entrance of a station.

"Excuse me" said Emma to a woman that was rushing past them, "Which station is this?"

"Victoria" the woman said as she disappeared into the station. "Come on" said Emma again. They followed the woman down the steps. "Last time I saw Meg we worked out that my Nan was trying to tell us something about Victoria station, that must be why we've ended up here"

Lucy shook free of Emma's grip on her arm and stood still. "Wait a minute" she said, "What's your Nan got to do with anything?" People were tutting and pushing past them, and they were getting jostled about.

"I told you it was a long story" Emma said, "Let's find somewhere to sit and I can try to explain it to you." She knew that explaining things would be nearly impossible to do, but they sneaked past the platform guard and she tried her best.

As Emma talked, several trains thundered into the station, then thundered out again. Emma looked up each time to see if Meg was getting off any of them, but she couldn't see her anywhere. The platform seemed to get busier and busier. Everyone was in a hurry and everyone was wearing dull coloured clothes and hats. Emma couldn't think why she had been able to come here tonight, without Meg and without any clue as to where she was. Surely Victoria station was where she was led to? Had she got it wrong?

She finally finished speaking. To her credit, Lucy hadn't interrupted once, even when Emma was telling her about when Meg turned up at Zoe's house during the birthday sleepover, or when she was explaining how they had cracked the various coded messages, or, indeed, when she had told her all about her Nan's crossword hints.

Lucy sat back with a huge sigh. "So how come we're here tonight when this Meg is nowhere to be seen" Lucy had decided to accept what Emma had been telling her, without asking any questions. What could she ask anyway? She would wake up at home soon and it would be the beginning of Thursday all over again. But while she was having such a vivid dream, she might as well run with it, and see where else it would take her.

"I don't know" said Emma, "I've never been here without her before, I can't understand where she can be".

"Unless this is part of a code too" said Lucy.

"What do you mean?" said Emma, sounding slightly put out that Lucy had started talking of codes when it really wasn't her adventure to speak of in such a way.

"Well, maybe she brought you here because she's in trouble and this is her sending you a message to help her." Lucy said, with a bit of a flourish. "You said that Victoria was part of your Nan's crossword, what exactly did it say?"

"I can't really remember," Emma said, "When I saw the word Victoria, I thought it was a name not the station," she desperately tried to think what the next clue had said on the crossword. "I think it said above or below or something like that" think Emma, think. "No! it said behind, that was it, it said behind and then a nonsense word that wasn't a word at all" Emma looked pleased with herself, but when she looked at Lucy, her pleasure faded a bit. Lucy was looking more confused than ever.

Another train tore into the station and into their thoughts. More people got off and rushed out of the station. "I think we should have a look around the station" said Lucy. "We're getting nowhere just sitting here". They followed the crowds and headed towards the station concourse. There were ticket barriers, a little stall selling snacks, a boy sitting at the feet of a man, shining his shoes and lots of people milling about. Emma looked around, trying to spot Meg or any clue as to where she might be. Her eye caught sight of a small queue of people waiting to buy their tickets from a ticket machine. The machine had a big sign on it, Ticket Vending Machine. The T, V and M were a bright blue that really stood out, and it suddenly occurred to Emma that she had seen those letters before.

"Lucy!" Emma suddenly said, "TVM!" She pointed at the ticket machine. "Nan's crossword, I remember what came after the word behind, it was TVM"

"Ticket Vending Machine" Lucy read, "Behind the Ticket machine?" She hurried over to the queue of people to get a closer look, Emma close behind her. They couldn't really get very close so Emma joined the queue and waited in line for it to move and take her closer to have a look.

Emma looked around as she waited in the queue. The station had obviously suffered some bomb damage and was looking a little worse for wear. But it was still busy and running as well as it could. Everyone looked so smart – no jeans and hoodies here and definitely no one plugged into their earphones. Everyone was just rushing about with newspapers tucked under their arms or checking their watches or holding umbrellas. No one was checking their phones or updating their situation on the latest social networking site, no one was talking loudly into their phones about what time they'd be home. It was quite refreshing to see people without a screen pressed to their face or ear.

Suddenly, Emma caught sight of a familiar face. She nearly missed Snow as he dashed past her, but she recognised his face, even though it was just a glimpse of profile. She almost called out, but she held back. What would Meg do? Eyes open, mouth shut. She watched him, weaving through the crowd towards the exit, then pause at the top of the steps, before turning left and disappearing.

"Lucy" Emma called. Lucy was looking at a magazine on the newsstand nearby. "Lucy, take my place in the queue, I'll be back in a minute".

Lucy put down the magazine and walked quickly over towards Emma, "Where are you going?" she said.

But Emma was already moving towards the exit. "Back in a minute" she said over her shoulder.

When she got to the top of the steps it struck her again how dark it was outside. She turned left and walked a few metres until she saw a man up ahead. "Where are you going?" she muttered under her breath. He wasn't too far away and she could see a lit cigarette in his hand. As he raised it to his mouth to take a drag, Emma could see his face more clearly. It was definitely Snow, and he was definitely slowing down. He came to a sudden stop, so Emma did the same. She hoped that the darkness was camouflaging her ok. She was glad that the school uniform she was wearing was black and grey and that her white school shirt didn't show too much under her V-neck jumper.

Snow looked up and down the street then darted to his left and opened a door. Emma rushed over to where he'd disappeared and saw a wooden door in the wall but there were no signs to show where it went. She looked around for clues. She hadn't walked very far from the station entrance at all. Could this door be a part of the station still?

Emma hurried back to where she'd left Lucy – Lucy was only one person away from the TVM, she beckoned urgently over to Emma. "Look" she said when Emma reached her. She was pointing to a door behind the ticket machine. It had the words Private on it in marker pen, but there were no station guards around making sure it stayed that way.

Emma and Lucy looked at each other and seemed to know what the other one meant by just a faint smile and a nod. As Lucy pretended to search for change, Emma slipped behind the machine and tried the door handle. To her surprise it opened straight away and she stepped through it and into a corridor. She closed it quickly behind her.

She stood in an echoey passageway. It was really cold, and the faint noises of the station could be heard, murmuring away behind the door. Emma felt scared, but quite excited. She missed Meg's efficient reassurance but she was sure she could do this without her.

Meg would be proud of her for solving the clues and finding this place. But what was this place? Suddenly, the door opened again. Emma whirled round, her heart in her mouth. It was Lucy.

"You nearly gave me a heart attack" Emma said.

"I couldn't let you leave me out there on my own" said Lucy, she smiled, a little unsteadily.

Emma composed herself. Poor Lucy, she'd only come round to listen to music and talk about school, and now look what had happened! To be fair, Lucy had been the chattiest and most animated Emma had ever seen her and, after this, Emma was sure they'd be better friends than they had been.

Emma and Lucy walked down the corridor, their footsteps echoing, even though they tried to walk on their tiptoes. There were no other doors that they could see so they just kept walking until they came to a dead end.

Emma felt that defeated feeling of disappointment. She was sure this was what her Nan had meant. They must've missed something.

"We must've missed something" she said out loud to Lucy.

They retraced their steps back to the door they'd come through. Just before they reached it, they heard a man's voice from the other side of the wall.

"Listen" Emma said

They stopped and held their breath.

"You told me that there were eyes on Cloud and that Hail had been taken in for questioning" the voice said.

"Do you recognise the voice?" Lucy said in a loud whisper.

"No, not really" said Emma, "But it must be Rain. He's talking about Cloud and Hail so it must be him".

"The one who is AWOL?" said Lucy

"Shhh! Yes" said Emma.

A woman's voice was talking now.

"Hail had come to my flat to warn me about you" it said.

"That's Meg!" said Emma, feeling a mix of relief that she sounded normal, and frustration, that she couldn't see how to reach her.

Lucy pressed her ear closer to the wall and felt around for any clue to how to get through it. Emma thought about the films she had seen and how it was usually a secret handle or a fake light fitting that opened the hidden door, but there was nothing but smooth wall.

A third voice spoke. "We still have Hail and we're still tracking Cloud. We believe that he is the one who is trying to pass on the co-ordinates to the Abwehr". The voice faded into a whisper that Emma couldn't quite catch.

"Who's that?" said Lucy, a little too loudly. "Shhh!" said Emma again. "I think it's Snow"

"The boss?" said Lucy, "Well, that's a good thing, isn't it?" She had given up looking for a secret door and had sat down on the floor, her back against the wall.

"I think so" said Emma, but she felt a bit uneasy. "Come on, I think I know how to get to that room now."

She led Lucy back through the door they'd come through, and tried to look as innocent as possible as they walked back into the station. They went out the exit and up the steps as quickly as possible, half expecting a guard to call after them, and ask them what they had been doing.

Out in the dark night they turned left and Emma quickly found the door that Snow had disappeared into. They hurried inside and found themselves in another corridor but this one had a door at the end.

"They're all in there" said Emma, but she made no move to go in.

"What's the matter?" asked Lucy, "Let's go in"

Emma hesitated. What was she waiting for? All the good guys were in there, they seemed to know that Cloud was the traitor, surely all they had to do now was stop him from getting the co-ordinates to Germany before the Operation began. And yet, something was niggling her. She couldn't quite put her finger on it. She pressed her ear to the door. She could hear Meg's raised voice.

"Well, where is he then? You said you had eyes on him, let's go and get him!" She sounded quite cross.

"It's not as easy as that" It was Snow's voice now. "We don't want to alert him until we can get solid proof that it really is him, we have to wait for him to make a move. Don't worry, we're watching him, it's all under control".

Lucy was still looking at Emma, waiting for the sign that it was ok to go in.

"Alright then, in we go" said Emma, "But I'd better go in first, Meg and Snow know me, they don't know you, I don't want them shooting you or anything".

Emma opened the door, but inevitably, it opened out onto her own landing. She needn't have worried about gunfire at all.

Chapter Fourteen

Meg felt uneasy about Snow's plan as soon as she got back to her own flat. She'd felt certain they'd got the right man when they were all discussing it in the room behind Victoria Station, but now severe doubts were creeping in.

When she looked at what she thought she knew, there wasn't really very much that made her feel like she knew anything! Rain had sent two notes and he was sure that Cloud was going to try and sabotage Operation Neptune by sending the co-ordinates to Germany.

The origin of the note that implicated Hail was still unclear, but he was in custody anyway, so couldn't do anything. When Hail had been in Meg's flat, he had said that Rain was the one planning the sabotage. Cloud had also said it was Rain when he'd spoken to Meg and Emma at the air raid shelter. Snow had said that he had eyes on Cloud so he must know that Cloud had spoken to Meg.

And Snow had now come out and agreed with Rain that Cloud was the traitor! Meg would've thought that Snow would arrest Cloud straight away and put an end to it once and for all. But Snow had been adamant that they needed more evidence. Since when did MI5 need evidence to arrest someone?

Meg sat down on her bed and kicked off her shoes. God knows where Florrie thought she'd been tonight – she'd missed her shift and left her right in the lurch. She would have to think up a good excuse by tomorrow morning. Meg looked at herself in the mirror, her face was pale, her lipstick all rubbed off now and her eyes gave away the anxiety she felt throughout her entire body. No way could she sleep tonight. She glanced at the bedside clock- five past five, she gave a sigh and lay back on her pillow. She couldn't be bothered to change into her nightgown or brush her teeth. She'd have to be up in a few hours. What was the point?

So, the plan was in place. Snow had given Meg and Rain strict instructions and, hopefully, by this time tomorrow it would all be over. Time was running out for Cloud, Operation Neptune was due to begin on Monday, it was now Thursday morning. If he was to get a message to Berlin he would have to send it soon. And if the message was sent over the wires, the code crackers at Bletchley would be on to it as fast as lightening. No, Cloud would have to take the message there, to Germany, himself.

Snow's theory was that Cloud would catch a train down to the coast and have a boat waiting for him there to take him across the Channel. Cloud had said that Rain would be catching a train from St Pancras to Dover, had he used him as a smokescreen to cover up his own intentions? Had he thought that Meg and Snow would be chasing down Rain and allow him, Cloud, to sneak off to Germany without detection?

He'd nearly convinced everyone too. Meg looked at the clock again, 5.07am. Something still wasn't sitting right in Meg's brain. It all seemed a bit too implausible. Cloud sounded utterly convinced that Rain was planning the betrayal and that Rain would be the one travelling down to Dover. If Cloud had been planning the same journey why would he point them in the direction of St Pancras at all? The train for Dover would be leaving there tonight.

So, the plan. It seemed straight forward enough. Snow, Rain and Meg would be waiting for Cloud at St Pancras and arrest him just as he was heading for the Dover train. That way there would be proof and it would be three against one in a very public place. Cloud would have no choice but to come quietly and his plan to sabotage Operation Neptune would be over. Churchill himself may even ring to congratulate them on a job well done.

And yet. And yet? Meg felt she was missing something. 5.10am. Why was time going so slowly? And where was Emma? Why hadn't she appeared last night? Meg thought that she could really do with a sounding board right now.

Meg rolled over on to her front and pushed herself up to sitting. There really was no point even trying to get to sleep. She got up and put the kettle on the stove. She would see dawn come up and with the sun rising, maybe her mind would clear and whatever it was that was niggling her would rise to the surface too.

After Emma and Lucy had returned to Emma's house it was getting too late to unpick what had just happened. The evening was getting on and Emma would soon be called downstairs for her tea.

"Well, I s'pose I'll see you tomorrow then" said Emma as she saw Lucy to the front door. Lucy stared at Emma. "I really don't know what to say" she said, "Not what I expected when I said I'd come home with you after school today!" They both burst out laughing.

"What's so funny, you two?" Diana said as she appeared at the front door.

Emma stopped laughing as she took in her mum's pinched expression, "How's Nan?" she asked.

"Oh, no change really" said Diana, with a weak smile, "Hello Lucy, have you two been having a nice time?"

Lucy had gone back to her usual mute self. She nodded then mumbled "see you tomorrow" to Emma and scampered out the door.

"She's such a funny girl" said Diana, and walked in to the house, "Come on Em, let's see what your dad has made us for tea."

"How's your new best friend?" Lea asked when Emma walked into the form room the next day. It was Friday and Emma was tired after yesterday and just wanting the day to be over so she could get back to Meg.

Lea didn't wait for an answer to her rather sarcastic question, she'd already turned to Zoe and Sarah and was chatting and laughing loudly. Emma chose not to rise to the bait. Zoe gave her an apologetic smile. Really it was Zoe who had been friends with Lucy since they were babies, so it was silly for Lea to be so cruel about her. Emma looked around the room, no Lucy yet. She must be tired after yesterday too. Emma hoped she hadn't said anything to anyone. She hadn't told her not to, but she assumed that Lucy wouldn't. There was no time to think about it anyway, the bell rang for registration and Miss Ross marched in.

Emma could get away with being quiet in lessons at the moment. All the staff knew that her Nan was unwell and they had taken it upon themselves to leave her alone, just give her a sympathetic smile every now and again. She sat in Maths with an empty seat beside her, still no Lucy.

At break time, Lea, Zoe and Sarah went off to the furthest corner of the playground to eat their crisps and Emma was, once again left on her own. It really wasn't turning out to be a very good day. If only she had Lucy to talk things over with. She was also feeling a bit guilty at not giving enough thought to her Nan. She would take a book with her when she visited her after school today, and read to her for a bit. Her mum had said that she was sure Nan could still hear them, even though she had been unconscious for nearly three days now.

The rest of the day passed quite quickly. Lunchtime was a bit awkward. Emma sat with the Lea and the others but nobody spoke much, then Emma had Spanish club so she went off to that for the rest of the hour. The last lesson on a Friday always takes the longest but it was Biology and the class got to watch a film about photosynthesis for most of it so everyone just fell asleep in the dark. It was quite a shock when the bell went and Miss Mullholland snapped on the lights and dismissed the class.

Lucy hadn't been in school all day but as Emma turned the corner into her road she saw a familiar figure sitting on the front wall outside her house. Lucy jumped down as Emma got closer. "Alright?" she said, pulling her earphones out so she could hear Emma's reply.

"Where were you today?" Emma asked.

"I just didn't feel like school" Lucy said, she didn't elaborate so Emma just shrugged.

"Neither did I really" she said. "I wish I hadn't bothered". As if Emma would ever dream of bunking off school!

"I've been waiting for you," Lucy said "You know, just in case you wanted to hang out again, like, er, like yesterday?"

Emma smiled. She really liked Lucy. She was funny and awkward and, yes, a little weird, but she seemed genuinely nice, just a bit shy. "I would really like to" said Emma, "But I've got to go and visit my Nan at the hospital. Shall I call for you after?"

Lucy looked a little flustered. "Oh, right, no, s'ok, I'll call for you, just text me when you're back" and she quickly walked away, stuffing her earphones into her ears as she went.

Emma tried to read her book out loud as she looked at her Nan breathing heavily and slowly next to her. It was quite disconcerting, reading to an inert audience with her parents and brother sitting nearby chatting quietly about Owen's football prowess. She stopped and cleared her throat. She lent close to her Nan's ear.

"Nan, can you hear me" she whispered, "I'm not sure how or what you know, but I worked it out. I found the room behind the ticket machine at Victoria. I just thought you should know. I think it's nearly over" Emma wasn't sure what she was expecting. She wasn't even sure how her Nan knew what was going on with her and Meg, but there was no way of knowing. Not for the first time recently, Emma felt a wave of sadness that she was so ill.

"Carry on, Em" said Diana, "I'm sure it's helping, she loves being read to."

Emma looked back at her book and carried on with "Carrie's War" – how ironic that the book she was reading for her English class was about a mystery set in the Second World War.

After half an hour, and sandwiches for tea, it was time to get back home.

"I think we need to say goodbye now" Diana said, her voice thick with grief. And everyone knew what she meant. There really wasn't much to say. Everyone knew that Nan loved them and Nan knew they all loved her but they each said it to her again, and kissed her cheek before filing out of the room for which was probably the last time.

Emma texted Lucy on the way back from the hospital. It was very quiet in the car. Diana had spoken to the doctor while Emma had been reading, it wasn't clear what was being said but Emma could tell from the body language that it wasn't good news. The doctor had tilted his head to one side as he'd said something in a low voice, and he had touched Diana's arm as she had put her head down in response. Emma's text had said that Lucy shouldn't come round, everyone was too sad about Nan. Emma half hoped that Lucy would ignore it and come round anyway. She felt sure that they'd get to see Meg tonight and she had really liked having someone from 2015 to talk to about it.

Emma needn't have worried. As the car turned into the driveway Lucy was sitting on the front wall again (or still?).

"Don't worry" said Emma to her mum, "It'll probably be a question about homework or something. I'll just have a quick chat with her then follow you in". She jumped out the car and headed over towards Lucy, who had now jumped down from the wall and was looking a little sheepish.

"How's your Nan?" Lucy asked as Emma walked up to her. She had taken out her earphones but Emma could hear the tinny rock music coming from them, dangling from her waist.

"No change" she said, "I read my English book to her".

"Carrie's War?" said Lucy, she couldn't hide the smile playing on her lips.

"I know!" said Emma, smiling back. "Listen, I'm not sure if my mum wants to have anyone round to play tonight, she's a bit upset and stuff"

Lucy's smile faded. "Oh, that's cool, no problem," she said, "Just, erm, just let me know what happens, yeah?" Emma really wanted Lucy to come in. She had a feeling that tonight some things would be resolved once and for all. Hadn't Cloud said that tonight was when Rain was planning to be at St Pancras? That was all up in the air now, of course, but something was going to kick off tonight, and Emma really wanted Lucy with her.

"Well, maybe just come in for a few minutes. I'm sure that would be ok"

Lucy and Emma went straight up to Emma's room when they got in the house. Emma felt quite excited as she opened her door, but when she looked inside, it was just her room. There was her bed with all her cuddly toys, there was her pyjamas hastily disguarded this morning. No sign of anything untoward. Lucy's face mirrored Emma's disappointment.

"Maybe I'll just go to the toilet" said Emma.

"Good idea" said Lucy.

96

Lucy heard the door shut and waited a few minutes. She listened and she walked out onto the landing. As she knocked on the bathroom door she hoped that Emma wouldn't answer.

"Won't be a minute!" said Emma through the door.

Lucy cursed under her breath. Emma was still in there then. She turned back to Emma's room to wait in there.

As she walked into the room a rush of air blasted into her face and Emma's room was no longer there. A bustling, noisy station concourse had taken its place. Not Victoria station, Lucy was sure of that, it was bigger and busier and full of people. Lucy was just wondering what she should do next when Emma appeared at her shoulder.

"Thank goodness you're here" said Lucy. "Where are we now?"

Emma looked around and didn't really see any clues as to which station they were in but she knew it must be St Pancras.

"Meg's here, I'm sure of it" and just as the words left her mouth, she spotted Meg with a short, blonde man, standing by the announcement boards. Emma was so relieved to see her that she strode over, forgetting all about Lucy. Lucy had to jog to keep up with her, fearing that she would lose sight of her amongst the crowds.

Meg caught sight of Emma as she bounded over to where Meg was standing with Rain. "So glad you could join us!" she said, "Where were you last night?"

Emma started to explain when she remembered Lucy standing by her side. She stopped talking, "This is Lucy, my friend from school" she said.

"Oh" said Meg, "and this is Rain" she gestured towards the blonde stranger next to her.

There was an awkward silence when everyone was thinking about how much everyone else knew about the situation.

Rain was the first one to speak. "Where's Snow? He said he'd be here."

Emma looked at Meg by way of an explanation. "Snow's theory is that Cloud will be catching a train from here tonight to try and make his way to Germany with the co-ordinates for Operation Neptune," she said.

"But I thought Cloud had told us Rain would be catching a train from here" said Emma.

Lucy shifted the weight from one foot to the other. "Why would Cloud tell us to come to the station to catch Rain when he was planning to come here to catch a train himself?" Lucy mumbled.

Everyone looked at Lucy. She was a little surprised at herself for letting her thoughts come out like that, but she was feeling a bit confused and had the sense that she was part of something very important.

"Where IS Snow?" said Rain again. He was looking increasingly agitated and kept checking his watch and looking up at the announcement board. "The Dover train leaves in ten minutes. We've got to get to the platform and see if Cloud turns up."

"Snow said we should wait for him here" said Meg, she checked her watch too and looked around the concourse. It was so busy it was hard to spot anyone.

"I really don't think we can wait any longer" said Rain. "We have to make sure that Cloud doesn't get on the train without us seeing him. Here" he thrust a platform ticket into Meg's hand, "we've got to go".

Meg turned to Emma and Lucy, "It's probably best if you two wait here. Just keep your eyes open, ok?"

Emma felt a bit of déjà vu. She remembered the first time she had heard Meg say that to her. Was it really less than a week ago?

Meg and Rain hurried off in the direction of the platform. Various men and women in uniform were heading in the same direction.

"What shall we do now?" said Lucy. Emma looked around at the crowds.

"Just keep our eyes open I suppose" she said.

They stood around for a few moments doing just that, when Emma suddenly saw a familiar figure running towards the platform barriers. He was still good looking, despite the suspicions that hung over him, there was no mistaking it, it was Cloud.

"Lucy!" said Emma in an urgent whisper, "It's Cloud. He's running to catch the Dover train, just like we suspected. Meg and Rain were right. He is trying to get to Germany with the co-ordinates!"

"Are you sure it's him?" said Lucy, craning her neck to see a man dashing through the barriers. He didn't even show a ticket to the guard. He soon disappeared from sight. "Come on!" said Lucy, "Let's go after him, just in case Rain and Meg miss him"

Emma and Lucy ran towards the platform but as they came to the barrier the guard stopped them, "Woah there young ladies! No-one passes onto the platform without a valid ticket to travel"

"Oh please let us through!" said Lucy, "My dad is leaving for France and I haven't had a chance to kiss him goodbye. I may never see him again" and to Emma's amazement, Lucy burst into tears. The guard looked hugely embarrassed and changed his tone immediately, "Oh now come on, don't cry dearie" he said, "of course I'll let you through" he stepped aside and the girls thanked him and rushed passed him, "Your dad's a hero!" he called after them.

Lucy's tears had miraculously disappeared just as quickly as they'd arrived. Emma was very impressed with Lucy's quick thinking and was just about to tell her so when they spotted Cloud, Meg and Rain up ahead having what appeared to be a very heated discussion. As they drew closer they heard Cloud, "I told you Rain was planning to catch the train to Dover, didn't I? And look, here he is!"

"Come on, Cloud" said Rain, "The game's up! We know it's you planning to get to Germany. You're here to catch the train, not me, you're just trying to put us off your scent"

Meg was standing by the side of them both looking like she was thinking hard.

"Just give it up Rain!" said Cloud, "You're not getting on this train so just come quietly. Meg! Come on! Help me arrest this traitor" He made a grab for Rain's arm, but Rain pulled away from him.

"Get off me" he said loudly, "You're not fooling anyone, Cloud. Meg! Tell him! Tell him we know everything and there's no way he's getting to Germany tonight"

"I'm not planning to go to Germany…"

"Just stop denying it now…

Rain and Cloud's argument was getting more and more heated. People were beginning to notice and stare as they got on the train around them. They had just begun to shove each other about a bit when Meg said in a quiet voice, "Where's Snow?"

Chapter Fifteen

Everyone stopped talking. Meg looked at Rain and Cloud and asked the question again, "Where's Snow?" Emma and Lucy looked at Meg. Nobody spoke as the same thought whirled through everyone's head.

The train suddenly gave a loud whistle as it prepared to depart. That seemed to break the tension a bit.

"But the evidence I gathered all pointed to you" Cloud said, gesturing towards Rain. "I showed Snow the letters you wrote to your brother and it all seemed to fall into place."

"How did you know about my brother in the Prisoner of War camp anyway?" Rain asked. "I mean, did someone tell you or did you just happen to find the letters?"

"Well, Snow told me initially, but he said it as a throw away comment. He said he didn't think it was relevant and you wouldn't be stupid enough to use that route to get to Germany." Cloud said.

"Snow told you?" said Emma. Cloud turned round to look at her for the first time since she'd arrived on the platform. The steam from the departing train swirled around him, making him look even more mysterious and handsome.

"What are you doing here?" he said.

"She's with me" said Meg, "Snow told you?"

Cloud looked back at Meg, "Yes, he said that Rain was missing so we had to find him. He was sure it was Rain who was the traitor."

"What did Snow tell you?" Lucy asked Rain. Cloud looked at Lucy, "Who are you?" he said. Lucy ignored him and continued to look at Rain.

"He didn't tell me anything really. He told me to find Cloud and keep my eye on him, just in case, but when I saw that Cloud was suspecting me I thought it must be Cloud that was the traitor so I tried to tell Meg"

"Through those notes." said Meg.

"Yes, exactly," said Rain, "I didn't want anyone else to work out what I thought I knew about Cloud, I knew Meg would be able to work out the codes."

"So, Snow told you both that the other one may be the traitor?" said Lucy. Cloud looked at her again.

"Who did you say you were again?" he said.

"I didn't" said Lucy.

Meg put her hands over her eyes and tried to figure out how to say out loud what she suspected everyone was thinking, including herself.

"Snow has played you off one another. He even wrote a note implicating Hail as a complete swerve ball. I think we all know who the traitor is now. Not some ex-German spy that we turned but one of our own – It's Snow!" she said.

Rain's face darkened. He looked at Cloud and they both nodded.

"We've got to stop him" said Rain. He felt that he'd been made a fool of. All that talk in Victoria last night. He hadn't doubted Snow for a minute. Some spy he was!

Cloud was having similar thoughts. He was convinced it was Rain that was going to betray them all. Now he would have to swallow his pride, apologise and work with him to find the real traitor in all this – Snow. "But we've no idea where he is" he said.

"Think" said Meg, "We know he has to go to Germany to take the co-ordinates to the Abwehr. He was the one who told us that sending them over the wires was not an option, the code-crackers in Bletchley would be on to it like a shot."

"So if he was going to the coast, why isn't he catching a train to Dover?" said Emma. Her head was aching from all the possibilities of what could happen.

"He wouldn't be that stupid. He's brought us all here on some wild goose chase so he has a clear run to get away" said Meg. She still looked up at the departure boards, even though she knew Snow wouldn't be anywhere near St Pancras station.

"There are other routes to the coast though, aren't there?" Everyone turned round to look at Lucy. She went a little red, "I mean, when I was about 6 we went to France on a holiday but we didn't get the ferry from Dover, we got it from Portsmouth and sailed across to Normandy."

Rain, Cloud and Meg all looked at each other. "Oh my goodness!" Meg said, "Portsmouth! Of course! He's due to be on one of the first boats out, to check out the landing sites – he told me that at the beginning of the search for the traitor. He would get to France easily, no questions asked."

"He's got some nerve!" said Rain, "Taking our secrets to Germany right under our noses"

"If it's true, of course" said Cloud, he didn't sound convinced.

"Well, do you have any other ideas?" said Lucy. She was feeling quite chuffed that her idea had been picked up and she didn't like Cloud doubting it.

Cloud scowled, "Who are you?" he asked for the third time. He didn't have any other ideas, of course, and he wanted to deflect the attention away from that.

Meg looked at the big clock in the station. "Look, we haven't really got time to discuss it. We have to try and stop him. If we're wrong then at least we can say we tried. We have to get to Victoria"

Emma and Lucy looked puzzled, "Why Victoria ?" they both said at once.

"Because trains to Portsmouth depart from there" said Meg as she briskly walked off towards the underground. Rain and Emma quickly rushed after her, leaving Cloud and Lucy to exchange one more glare at each other before hurrying along behind them.

It was only a short tube ride to Victoria but it seemed to take forever. There was no guarantee that they'd find anything when they got there but, as Meg had said, they all felt that they had to try.

No-one spoke as the train rumbled into Victoria, but they were all up and on their feet before the doors opened. They walked quickly to the over ground part of the station and found themselves, once again, peering at a departure board.

"There!" said Emma, rather too loudly, "Platform 7, train to Portsmouth"

"What's the time?" Meg asked, even though there was huge station clock just above the departure board. She answered her own question, "Ten past Seven" she said, "The train leaves in fifteen minutes"

"So, we wait?" said Emma.

"Yes, we wait" said Cloud, "and just keep our eyes open".

Emma and Lucy walked over to a bench and sat down, while the others stood around, trying not to look too suspicious. There were three trains to Portsmouth displayed on the board. It could be a long wait, Emma thought.

"I'll just go and get us some platform tickets" said Rain, checking his pockets for change.

"I'd better come with you" said Cloud. He obviously still had doubts about Rain and didn't want him out of his sight. Emma looked at Meg to see if she would go with them, but she seemed ok with it and was looking around the station for any sign of Snow.

The minutes ticked on. It didn't look like anyone was catching the 7.25 to Portsmouth. Nobody seemed to be heading towards platform 7 at all.

"Here" said Rain, handing out the tickets, "It's probably best if Meg, Cloud and I wait for Snow on the platform and Emma and her friend wait here".

Emma opened her mouth to protest, but Meg agreed with Rain, "Yes, Emma you stay here, we don't know how dangerous it will get when Snow sees that we're on to him, I'd hate anything to happen to you on my account, it's my fault you're here in the first place. Just stay here and wait, hopefully we'll be back with Snow before you know it."

"Oh please Meg" Emma began, "I'd be an extra pair of eyes, I could help…"

"No" said Meg firmly, "Stay here. Honestly, Emma, it's too dangerous. Come on you two" she turned to Rain and Cloud and all three of them marched off to Platform 7.

"Great!" said Emma, "Now I'll miss all the action. It's all been leading up to this and now I'll miss the final bit! It's not fair!" She sat down on the bench with a "harrumph". Lucy sat down again too. She didn't really know what to say. To her, this was all a big adventure. If they waited here or on the platform, she still couldn't quite believe where she was.

"What does this Snow look like?" she asked.

Emma shook herself out of her grumpy mood and tried to remember. She'd only met him once that night with Meg in the park, and it was very dark. "He's tall" she said.

"Well, that narrows it down a bit, I don't think!" said Lucy with a laugh.

Emma smiled, "Ok," she said, "I think he's got short brown hair"

"Oh well why didn't you say so?" Lucy said with a giggle, "That'll make him far easier to spot now that I know he has brown hair!"

"It was dark when I met him!" said Emma, a little crossly, "and he was wearing a hat. They all wear hats! Look around! It'll be impossible to spot him."

Lucy and Emma didn't say anything for a while. The station clock said twenty past seven. "It's getting a bit late now, maybe he's taking a later train?" said Lucy, breaking the silence. Emma nodded, but looked around to see if anyone was rushing towards the platform. Anyone who was tall, had brown hair and was wearing a hat.

Suddenly, out of the corner of her eye, Emma saw a man and a woman arguing as they walked towards one of the other platforms. Lucy noticed too and stood up to get a better view. As the couple got a little bit closer, she could hear a bit of what was being said. "I told you!" the woman was saying, "I don't know why he offered to buy me a cup of tea! There's nothing going on!" The man was holding the woman's elbow and steering her in the direction of platform 3. "Oh come on Shirley! He's had his eye on you for months, don't be so naïve!" They passed close by Lucy and Emma. Lucy looked round to Emma to see if she had heard the argument, but when she turned towards her, she was staring off in the complete opposite direction.

"Classic!" said Emma, as she started to walk quickly towards platform seven. Lucy hurried after her, "What?" she said as she caught up. "That argument? Between those two? It was a distraction!" said Emma. "I missed it once before, but not tonight!"

Lucy looked confused. "What?" she said again.

"When everyone was watching that couple arguing, a man rushed past us towards the Portsmouth train" said Emma

"Did he?" said Lucy, "Where?"

"Just up ahead" said Emma, doing a quick walk/run to get closer.

"The tall man in the hat?" said Lucy.

"Exactly!" said Emma, "Come on! He's getting on the train"

Emma and Lucy saw Snow disappear through one of the open train doors. Emma had a quick look around for Meg, Rain and Cloud but couldn't see them anywhere. Maybe they hadn't seen him, or maybe they were on the train already. Emma didn't really have time to think. The guard had brought the whistle to his lips and the train was about to go. Lucy and Emma swung onto the train through the same open door as Snow and shut it behind them.

Almost as soon as they were on, the train started slowly moving off. They were on their way to Portsmouth.

Chapter Sixteen

The train was like no other train that Lucy and Emma had been on before. Evidently smoking was allowed and the corridors were quite foggy with cigarette smoke. There were windows alongside one side and sliding doors into each of the compartments alongside the other. The corridor was empty when Emma and Lucy had turned round after slamming the train door shut behind them. Snow must be in one of the compartments, Emma thought. But which one? And would he recognise Emma if he saw her again?

Emma and Lucy walked along to the first compartment. Emma peered in but couldn't really see the faces of those inside. She carefully slid back the door, trying to make as little noise as she could. The compartment was full. Two men in uniform were sitting opposite each other, they were fast asleep with their heads leaning on the window. There was a couple of women who were both rummaging in their hand bags for hand mirrors, lipsticks, powder or whatever. Lucy felt like telling them not to bother, the soldiers looked like they would be asleep all journey. Besides, the women were by far the most beautiful she'd seen this adventure. Hair that was set rigid in a curled under sort of style and bright red pouty lips that any celebrity from one of Lucy's magazines would've paid good money for.

The other four seats were taken up with a family of sorts. It looked like grandparents with the two young children. There was a worried look on the granny's face and the grandpa was getting out a book to read to the children. All, except the sleeping soldiers, looked up as Emma and Lucy peered in. No Snow in here then. Emma gave a faint smile before pulling her head back into the corridor and sliding the door shut again.

"One down" said Emma, "onto the next one". They walked a little but further down and tried the next compartment. There were a few empty seats in this one. Three men, all in uniform. They obviously were enjoying the space and glared at Emma and Lucy, daring them to try and sit down and ruin their journey. "Sorry" said Emma, she often apologised when she felt uncomfortable. She slid the door shut and they moved on to the next one.

"Listen" said Lucy, "This could take forever. I'll go on ahead to and do every other compartment, we'll find Snow quicker"

"But you don't know what he looks like" said Emma, "We'd better stick together"

"Tall, brown haired man, with a hat, travelling alone, probably looking suspicious, I think I'll be able to recognise him" said Lucy, already taking off down the corridor, leaving the nearest compartment for Emma.

Emma admired Lucy's impulsiveness at times, but she was not sure about it in this instance. But it was too late to call after her now, she was already opening the door into the compartment. Emma did the same to the one nearest her.

It was really smoky inside and, again, there were empty seats. The only other passengers were a man and a woman who didn't seem to know each other. The woman was staring determinedly out the window and the man had raised a newspaper to read just as Emma had peeped in. So maybe they do know each other after all, thought Emma, I've definitely just interrupted something. She mumbled an apology and ducked out back into the corridor.

She saw Lucy up ahead who gestured a shrug to her. She hadn't found Snow either. "Next one" Emma said to herself.

As soon as she slid back the door to the compartment she knew that she'd found him. There were two men in there and one was looking right at her as soon as her face appeared in the doorway. Before Emma had a chance to wind her head in and call to Lucy from the corridor, Snow was up like a flash. He grabbed her hard by the arm and yanked her into the compartment.

"You?" he said with a snarl. "Where's Meg?" he tightened his grip on Emma's arm.

"Ow!" said Emma, "Let go of me, you're hurting me!" she struggled against his grip, but he was way too strong. Emma wondered why the other passenger didn't step in to help, but she couldn't twist herself round to see where he was. Snow didn't let go, but brought his face even closer to hers.

"Not until you tell me where Meg is" he said.

Emma felt the panic rising up in her. Meg had been right. It was far too dangerous for her, she should've stayed in the station. Was Meg even on the train? What would she do if she wasn't?

"She'll be here any minute" she said with, what she hoped, was confidence. "And she's not alone. Rain and Cloud know what you've been up to as well. They'll all come bursting in any minute now."

Snow and Emma both looked at the open door. Nobody was bursting in anywhere any time soon. Snow dragged Emma back towards the door and slid it shut.

He loosened his grip a little and shoved her down onto one of the seats. He was sweating quite a lot and looked a little pale. "Now what am I going to do with you?" he said. Emma wasn't sure if it was a rhetorical question or not, so she didn't answer. Besides, she didn't think "Let me go" would've been the answer he was looking for.

"Who the hell is that?" said the other man. Emma had almost forgotten he was there, he'd been so quiet.

"One of Meg's little friends" said Snow. "I'd hoped that they'd all be at St Pancras still, tying themselves into knots about who the traitor was. I suppose I trained them too well, they worked it out far too easily."

"I told you!" said the other man, "If you'd arrested Rain and Cloud like I said you should, Meg would've left well alone. Now it looks like they'll all be here any minute"

It slowly dawned on Emma who this man was. It was Hail, it had to be. Despite Meg telling her that Snow had arrested him when he appeared at Meg's flat a few nights ago, and despite the "graupel" note, which somehow didn't fit, Hail was working with Snow and they were both heading to Germany with the co-ordinates.

"Hail" she said out loud. Hail looked startled. "You're Hail, aren't you?"

Hail turned to Snow, "What are we going to do with her? How are you going to shut her up all the way to Portsmouth?" Hail looked at Emma again. He had small eyes and a scowly face, but that might just be because of his current mood. His moustache was well groomed and he was very blonde and very tall. His accent was still quite strong but he was wearing the uniform of an eccentric British

109

gentleman. Dark suit with a spotty, silk cravat and Emma noticed a briefcase and an umbrella in the luggage rack above his head.

"This might help" said Snow, producing a handgun from his jacket pocket and pointing it at Emma.

Emma sat rigid and a bit more upright than before. Hail had taken out his gun too and he was showing it to Snow. Emma looked towards the door to see if there was any hope of making a run for it, but it was too far away and too fiddly to slide it across and get out without imagining two bullet holes in the back of her head.

Suddenly, Lucy's face appeared at the door. Emma tried to tell her with her eyes to not come in. Lucy's own eyes widened when she saw Emma with two men who were evidently waving a couple of guns around.

Lucy's face disappeared quickly and Emma allowed herself a little sigh of relief, before realising her predicament again. She hoped Lucy had found the others and that they'd know what to do. If she didn't it would be a long ride to Portsmouth, and that's only if she made it that far.

Lucy stood back against the windows just outside the compartment where Emma was being held. She took a few deep breaths then composed herself. She would have to find Meg, Rain and Cloud, they'd know what to do. It hadn't occurred to her that they might not be on the train. They had to be, otherwise she had absolutely no idea what she would do.

She started her compartment by compartment search again. This time looking for Meg and the others, and not missing out every other one. She just hoped that Snow and whoever that other man was, wouldn't do anything stupid in the meantime.

As she walked further and further away from Emma, she really began to panic. She checked her watch, ten to eight. She wondered if the time was the same back in 2015. Her mum wouldn't notice she was still out yet anyway. She wouldn't notice for hours, if at all. Lucy fixed her mind back to the job in hand. Just as she was on her third compartment she noticed a woman quite far up ahead who appeared to be doing the same thing, checking compartments.

"Meg" Lucy said quietly. She hurried towards her. She was quite close by the time Meg noticed her and the look of Meg's face read relief and worry at the same time.

"Where's Emma?" was the first thing she said when Lucy reached her.

"Snow's got her" said Lucy, "they're in a compartment down there" she pointed down the corridor, "and there's another man in there too"

"What?" said Meg, "Snow's not alone?" She was just digesting this news when Rain and Cloud appeared behind her. They had appeared in a puff of smoke almost, the door which they'd opened had let out a cloud of cigarette smoke. Lucy would've laughed under other circumstances, but when she saw the look on Meg's face, it was driven home how serious the situation was.

"Snow's got someone with him" Meg said, turning round to Rain and Cloud, "And he's got Emma"

"That sneak Hail!" said Rain, "It has to be him. He's always been greasing up to Snow and now we know why, they're in it together"

"Hail has all the contacts" Cloud chipped in, "It must be him. They've both been trying to frame us, and throw us off course with that extra note and Hail's arrest. Blast it! I should've seen it coming"

Cloud and Rain looked thunderous.

"What about Emma?" said Lucy, when she finally found her voice again. "We've got to get her out of there."

Cloud looked at Lucy. He had disliked her from the first time he'd met her earlier that evening and the look he gave her seemed to confirm this dislike even more.

"That stupid girl!" he said, "Both of you! You were told to stay where you were and leave it to us! Why couldn't you do as you were told?" he turned to Meg, "They have made it ten times more difficult to arrest Snow now, all because they wanted some adventure and excitement! Well, let me tell you little girl" he looked back at Lucy, "This is not a game! This adventure could kill us all! Happy now?" he banged the window with his fist and turned away, not being able to look at Lucy any longer.

There was a beat or two of silence, before Meg brought a bit of common sense to proceedings. "Alright Cloud, calm down a bit, what's done is done. We have to deal with the situation as it is now. I don't think even Snow would want a shoot out on a moving train full of civilians."

"What about Hail though?" said Rain, he had been looking just as angry as Cloud, but now sounded a steely sort of calm. "Hail is unpredictable, I've worked with him for years, both here and when we were in Germany"

Meg hadn't forgotten that Hail, Rain and Cloud were all German, but it always gave her a little jolt when someone referred back to their Germany days, spying for the enemy. She shook her head to make room for some clear thoughts about what to do.

"Right" she said, "Lucy. Did Snow or Hail see you?"

"No, I don't think so" Lucy said, "They were too busy looking at the guns they had turned on Emma"

"They've got their guns out already?" said Rain, "They can't even handle a little girl without getting their guns out?" He turned to Meg, "This doesn't bode well, Meg, what are we going to do? Wait until Portsmouth?"

Meg thought for a bit. It wasn't ideal, but she couldn't put Emma through the long journey to Portsmouth with two guns pointing at her the whole way. "No" she said, "we've got to do something before then. We can't risk them getting out at Portsmouth and disappearing with Emma."

Lucy looked alarmed. "Can I do something? They don't know me, they don't even know I'm here, can't I help?"

Cloud looked Lucy up and down. "They might not know you" he said, "But you're wearing the same school uniform as Emma. It doesn't take an international spy to work out that you're Emma's friend!"

Lucy blushed. How could she think that she'd be of any help at all? It was beginning to look a little hopeless.

Meg tried again, "Ok, so we know which compartment they're in and that Snow has Hail with him. We know that they have guns and they will do anything to get to Germany to deliver the co-ordinates"

"Tell us something we don't know" said Cloud, scowling again.

Meg ignored him. She was about to open her mouth to speak again when a compartment door slid open and a young woman appeared. She looked a little surprised to see such a gathering in the corridor but she walked past them and headed off to the refreshment carriage.

"We shouldn't be talking out here" said Meg, "Let's go back to our compartment and discuss what to do there".

Once inside, Meg slid the door safely behind them. "We have to get to Emma and let her know we're here, she must feel so frightened"

"It's her own fault" said Cloud,

"Shut up!" said Meg and Lucy at the same time. "Your negative comments are being no help whatsoever, so keep it shut until you have something useful to say" Meg had really told him off. Cloud looked suitably embarrassed.

"The train is due to arrive in Portsmouth at about 11 o'clock so we have just over three hours to arrest Snow and Hail and rescue Emma" said Meg. "The train we're on has a refreshment carriage and two WCs."

Lucy must've looked blank, Meg explained that WCs were toilets and continued with her deliberations. "There is a long corridor alongside the compartments so there is only one door to get out of when the train is in motion. When the train stops at a station there are doors that open out straight onto the platform as well."

Rain and Cloud were following it all and wondering where Meg was going with all this. Meg was just setting out the information they had, hoping that a plan would formulate as she went along.

"Does the train stop at other places before Portsmouth?" asked Lucy.

"Only once, at Woking" said Meg "and that will be in about half an hour's time".

"Can we get out and get into Snow's compartment when we stop then?" said Lucy.

Cloud rolled his eyes, "We can get into the compartment from the corridor any time we like" he said, with scorn in his voice, "from the corridor side".

Lucy gave him the most withering look she could manage under the circumstances, "I know that, thank you, but I was thinking that it would be better, and more surprising, if we burst into the compartment via two entrances, rather than one. Seeing as there are two of them and they wouldn't expect it as much, ok?" she looked back at Meg to see if she was thinking along the same lines.

"Yes" said Meg, a little distractedly, "I think you might have the bare bones of a plan there. But it still doesn't get rid of the fact that Snow and Hail have got their guns out already and that they are so close to completing their plan to wreck what could be one of the most important turning points to end this war"

Everyone was silent for a few moments. The rattle and shake of the train lulling them all from side to side as they thought of a distraction to make Snow and Hail put their guns away and be wrong footed when Meg and the others burst into their compartment at Woking.

"What if" Rain began, "the ticket inspector happened to be inspecting their tickets right at the moment when the train is getting into Woking station?" he looked up at Meg with a hopeful look on his face. Lucy was pleased to see that Meg was the one taking charge. She had learned enough about history to know that a woman in charge of any job was pretty unusual.

"Good idea" Meg said, "but I don't see how we can do that. It is very unlikely that the real ticket inspector would do that and even if you or Cloud could get hold of a ticket inspector's uniform, they would recognise you like a shot"

"They wouldn't recognise me" said Lucy

Cloud was about to open his mouth and say something negative again, when Lucy interrupted him and continued, "I mean, I could disguise myself as a female ticket inspector, they do have them nowadays, don't they?"

"Since the war began, more and more" said Meg with a slight smile on her lips.

"Well then, let me have a go" said Lucy

"But you look so young..." Cloud began. Lucy whipped out a mascara and eyeliner that she always carried in her skirt pocket. Meg saw what she did and grabbed her bag and pulled out a head scarf and a lipstick.

"It must be worth a go" said Rain doubtfully.

"Is this the only plan we have?" asked Cloud.

114

Meg looked at Lucy, "It's going to be awfully dangerous" she said, "Are you sure you want to do this?"

Lucy didn't' even hesitate, "Of course" she said, "Emma would do exactly the same thing for me"

"Ok then" said Meg, snapping into business mode, "Rain, you go out and see if you can find the ticket inspector's quarters. Tell them you need a uniform immediately for King and country" Rain got up, "Flash them your gun and they'll understand" Meg added as he slid open the door. "Cloud, you go and hover in the corridor, make sure no one comes out of Snow's compartment"

"It's the fifth one down" Lucy said as he followed Rain out the door.

"Now for you" Meg said,"Let's start with your make- up" and she unscrewed her lipstick, "We've got about twenty minutes".

Chapter Seventeen

It was coming up to half eight when Diana got the phone call from the hospital. She knew as soon as the phone rang that it couldn't be good news. The voice at the other end told her to come back to the hospital at once, it looked like this was going to be it.

Diana put the phone down and sat down at the kitchen table to gather herself. She wouldn't tell Emma and Owen yet, they were upstairs playing with Emma's friend Lucy or doing homework, so she thought, there was no need to drag them back to the hospital tonight. Besides, they'd really said their goodbyes already. The old lady lying in the hospital bed wasn't really their Nan anymore. Diana wanted to leave them with the happy memories and not too many sad ones.

Richard came into the kitchen and when he saw his wife's face he didn't have to say anything. He gathered her up in a big hug, "I'll just pop next door and get Pat to come round and sit with the kids" he said.

Owen was the only 'kid' in the house, of course, but luckily Pat didn't bother going upstairs to check. She assumed that they were both in bed when she came round, Richard hadn't told her any different, so she kicked off her shoes and put the television.

Emma had relaxed marginally since Snow and Hail had put their guns away. Their hands were still resting on the pockets that they'd disappeared into but at least they weren't pointing at her now. She could only guess what was going on with Lucy and the others. She didn't even contemplate the idea that Meg wasn't on the train.

"What are we going to do with her?" Hail said again. He had spent the last fifteen minutes asking variations on that same theme. "We can't take her all the way to Portsmouth, it would take too much explaining"

Snow was still sitting next to Emma with a grip on her arm. "Well, we can't put her out at Woking" he said, "She'll raise the alarm and we'll never make it onto the boat."

Emma took some comfort in the fact that they probably wouldn't kill her before Portsmouth because a dead body would take a lot of explaining too and there really was nowhere to hide one anyway. She began to feel a new indignation grow in her, and a new confidence. How dare they grab her and treat her this way? It was against her basic human rights to be held hostage like this. Emma was sure there was some international law that said that.

"Can I go now?" she heard herself ask. Hail and Cloud looked at her with frowns deep in their foreheads. "I mean, you don't want to keep me here all the way to Portsmouth and you can't drop me off at the next stop, so why not just let me go?"

"Where's Meg?" Snow asked again.

"I honestly don't know" said Emma, "If she was on the train don't you think you'd have seen her by now? Don't you think she would've tried to rescue me?"

Hail looked as if he agreed but Snow was still frowning, "She's probably cooking up some plan along the corridor somewhere"

Emma hoped he was right.

"You forget that I've worked with Meg for over two years now, I know how she works, I taught her most of it, for goodness sake! No, if I know her at all I bet she's on this train right now and is somehow planning to sabotage our whole trip"

Snow looked so angry now, "I won't let her, I can't! we're so close! We just have to get to Germany tomorrow morning and give the co-ordinates. That'll give the Germans plenty of time to re organise and get down to Normandy, ready and waiting"

"And when Hitler wins" Hail chimed in, "There'll be rewards all round".

Emma almost expected him to give a comedy villainous laugh and rub his hands together. He didn't, of course, and the situation lurched towards the terrifying again. Where was Meg? Did she know what she was up against?

"There" said Meg, "all done!" Lucy wished she had a bigger mirror, but all she could see in Meg's powder compact was her bright red lips and her dark eyes. She tried to see what the headscarf looked like but she had to take Meg's word for it that it looked fashionable and grown up. Rain had brought back a huge ticket inspectors uniform, but with Meg's belt she had managed to make it almost fit. She had borrowed Meg's satchel too, which looked like one that an inspector would carry and she had put a notepad and pen in it, as well as her eyeliner, mascara and phone, for what reason, she wasn't sure.

"I have to admit, you look just like a grown up ticket inspector" Rain said, he looked at Cloud for back up.

"Yes, I suppose I have to admit it too" Cloud said, rather reluctantly.

"Ok," said Meg, feeling quite pleased with herself, "We've got about five minutes to go through it again. Lucy, tell me what you're going to do"

Lucy repeated the instructions that Meg had given to her earlier, "I'm going to knock on the door of the compartment just after the announcement that the train is now approaching Woking station"

"Good" said Meg, "Then what?"

"I am going to ask to see their tickets and make small talk about the weather and the war" said Lucy

"I'd steer clear of the war if I were you" said Rain, "You don't want to get their tempers up or say something obviously wrong"

"Ok, "said Lucy, "I will just talk about the weather and take my time looking at the tickets. Hopefully I can make that last until the train has stopped at the station."

"Not 'hopefully', you have to" said Cloud, with his usual negative slant on things.

Lucy just looked at him. The others went through their parts in the plan but just as Meg was repeating her bit the announcement came. "Ladies and gentlemen, the train will shortly be arriving at Woking station, please make sure you take all your belongings with you and, for your own safety, extinguish all cigarettes before leaving the train, thank you, we wish you a safe onward journey"

"Show time!" said Lucy,

"What?" said Meg

"Never mind" said Lucy, "I'm going. Wish me luck!"

Chapter Eighteen

"If you don't let me go to the toilet, I'm going to wet myself". Emma was fidgeting on the seat next to Snow. He wasn't holding on to her wrist anymore but he was keeping a close eye on her.

"We're just about to stop at Woking" he said, "You can't go to the toilet when the train's in a station, you'll have to wait"

"Well, you should've let me go when I asked about fifteen minutes ago!" Emma said, with a huff. She didn't really need a wee but she was getting fed up of waiting to be rescued, she needed to do something.

"Just be quiet now" said Hail. He looked like he might need the toilet himself, he kept getting up and pacing to the other side of the compartment then sitting down again. He also kept patting his pocket, presumably making sure his gun was still where he'd put it. He turned to Snow, "I really don't know how much longer I can bear her whining, can't we just chuck her out here? It will take her ages to find anyone to tell, and who's going to believe her anyway? A school girl? Saying that a British spy is going to Germany to warn the enemy of an important plan? Sounds very unlikely to me!" Hail sat down again.

The knock at the door and it sliding open interrupted Snow's reply.

"Evening!" said Lucy, in her most grown up voice, "may I see your tickets please", she sounded very posh, Emma would've laughed if she hadn't checked herself.

Snow looked a bit taken aback. The train was slowing to a halt at Woking station and he was obviously not expecting a ticket inspector to come round at this very moment. "Where's the other fellow? The one who came round earlier?" Snow said, looking at Lucy with a steely glare.

If Lucy was scared she was hiding it very well, "Oh he got a little bit of travel sickness. Always does, poor chap, I really don't know why he took this job when he travels so badly, but needs must, as they say, and everyone has to do their bit for the war effort, don't you agree?" Lucy gave her best smile, which looked massive with her red lips. It was hard not to smile along with her.

No one said anything after this little speech. The train was now almost at a complete halt. The steam was rising out the window as the wheels screeched. Everyone jolted as the train finally stopped. "So," Lucy said again, "May I see your tickets please?"

Snow got up to get his jacket from the luggage rack opposite where Emma was sitting, Hail reached inside his pocket. Emma half expected him to pull his gun out again but his hand re-emerged with his ticket, much to her relief. Lucy gave a cursory glance over Hail's ticket but Snow was still rummaging in his jacket when the door to the platform suddenly rattled and burst open. "Freeze!" yelled a familiar voice.

Meg was pointing her gun straight at Snow and Rain was pointing his at Hail. There was no sign of Cloud yet. Snow went to move. "I said freeze" Meg twitched her gun at Snow again, but he kept moving towards the seat where he'd been sitting just before. "Don't make me do this, Snow" Meg said as she pulled back the catch on her gun. Snow continued his slow movement towards Emma. "One more move and I swear I will shoot you!" Meg didn't look like she was messing about.

Snow obviously thought so too and finally stopped moving. He still had his jacket in his hands though, and was hovering between putting his hands all the way up in surrender and holding on to it.

"What are you doing, Meg?" Snow said. His voice sounded gentle and consoling as if he was her friend again. Meg didn't bat an eyelid. "Come on," Snow said, "What's your plan now? The train will be moving again soon, are you going to point that thing at me the whole way to Portsmouth?"

"You're not going to Portsmouth, Snow" said Rain, still pointing his gun at Hail. "Your journey stops here, we're getting off"

Hail suddenly did a quick turn and kicked Rain hard in the stomach. Rain clutched his stomach and bent double, he had managed to keep hold of his gun but it was no longer pointing at Hail, who had now grabbed hold of Lucy and was pointing his own gun straight into her ear.

"You've got to do better than that" said Hail. "You can take Snow, I don't care, I can go on without him, but I won't let you ruin our plan, we're too close now"

Snow looked a bit upset that Hail had sold him out so readily but there wasn't much he could do at the moment. Emma had got up and positioned herself behind Meg, and Rain had recovered himself and repointed his gun at Hail.

"Drop the gun, Hail" said Rain, "You can't do this, come on, we've known each other for so long, don't do this". Rain tried to appeal to him. "Remember, I know what it feels like to be captured, just like you, and I know how angry I felt to be asked to help the British against my beloved fatherland."

Meg looked a little alarmed at the word "fatherland" – that's what Hitler called Germany, but she thought she understood why he was talking like this. It was better than talking in German, like they could've done, of course, but she knew that Rain wanted her to understand what he was saying.

"But I also know that what I'm doing is right" Rain continued, "I believe that the war is nearly over and Operation Neptune is the catalyst. Please don't jeopardise it. Be loyal to what you swore you would do. Do you really want the war to continue? Do you really want all those soldiers' blood on your hands?"

Hail momentarily removed the gun from pointing at Lucy to give a sarcastic round of applause to Rain's speech. His snide smile abruptly changed to an angry scowl. "Traitor!" he spat the words out at Rain. "You don't know the meaning of the word 'loyal'. I've spent the last two years trying to find a way to get out of this mess and back to the country I love and am proud of. And now I have, and you're the one who is sending soldiers to their deaths, not me. You wait until they land on those beaches in Normandy. Do you really think they're just going to walk into France and take it back?"

"Of course not" said Rain, he was getting more and more angry. "But we'll lose a darn sight more men if you give the enemy the co-ordinates of where they'll be."

"The enemy?!" Hail laughed a cruel laugh, "Listen to you! You've well and truly turned haven't you?" He let his voice quieten a bit "I thought you'd understand" he paused, "I even thought you might join us"

Emma was listening to all this from behind Meg. She tried to catch Lucy's eye to reassure her in some way, but Lucy was actually looking quite calm, despite Hail's gun back at her temple.

"Ladies and Gentlemen, this train is getting ready to depart, please ensure you have all your belongings with you and please close all the doors." The announcement shook everyone into action.

"Rain, take Snow and Emma off the train, I'll deal with things this end" said Meg, bravely.

"I'm not going anywhere" said Emma. It was the first time she'd spoken in a while, and her voice came out in a bit of a croak. "I can't leave Lucy"

"Lucy?" said Hail, "So she's another one of your helpers is she?" he looked down at his hostage. "Well, that makes things a bit more interesting" he smiled and seemed to think himself very clever. If Emma and Meg cared so much about Lucy he would have a real bargaining tool to play with. He might get out of all this after all.

"No, you go" said Rain, "I can deal with this" he still had his eyes on Hail, but he turned slightly towards Meg, "I know him better than you, take Emma and Snow and I'll catch up with you later"

"I told you, I'm not going anywhere" said Emma again, a little louder, she hated being ignored.

Meg hesitated, she looked at Snow who was smiling at her, enjoying her dilemma of what to do. Meg's face hardened.

"Come on, Snow" she said, "You're out of here". She waved her gun at Snow and at the door out to the platform. As Snow walked towards her, she looked back at Hail, or just past his shoulder at any rate. The sliding door to the corridor was still open from when Lucy had come in earlier, and she could just make out Cloud's elbow hovering behind.

"And you, Emma, let's go" she said.

"No, I'm not leaving" Emma said, she walked away from Meg and towards where Hail was holding Lucy.

"Emma, no!" said Rain, "Don't go any closer, just stop where you are" His gun was still pointing at Hail but he managed to reach out and grab Emma, pulling her behind him.

123

"Rain, you'll have to take Snow" said Meg, "I can't leave the girls" Rain started to say something but she cut him off, "Honestly, Rain, you go. Raise the alarm and tell the authorities to meet the train at Portsmouth, I won't be on my own" she raised her eyebrows, hoping Rain would realise that she had meant Cloud was nearby.

Rain nodded, he prodded Snow in the back with his gun. Snow had little choice but to walk towards the door. He stepped down onto the platform and looked back at Hail. "Finish the job, Hail" he said, "I'm counting on you" and then he added, almost inaudibly, "Germany's counting on you".

"Get out!" said Rain behind him. Just as Rain's feet had reached the platform, Cloud burst into the compartment from the corridor side, he ran towards Hail and wrestled him to the ground.

Lucy sprung back and let out an involuntary scream as she saw that Cloud and Hail had their bodies pressed close together with the hands that held their guns pressed into each-others stomachs.

"Look out!" she shouted, Emma grabbed her and they held on to each other as Meg tried to aim her gun at Hail. It was very difficult to get a clear shot as Cloud and Hail writhed around on the floor. Snow and Rain were both on the platform as the commotion began but a guard had already shut the door behind them, there was nothing Rain could do now as the train began to pull away.

Back on the train the chaos continued. Lucy and Emma were trying to shout encouragement to Cloud and Meg but it was so difficult to see who was on top.

Suddenly a gun shot fired. The wrestling stopped abruptly and nobody moved.

Chapter Nineteen

"I'm sorry for your loss" the doctor had come over to talk to Diana as she sat by her ma's bed.

"She didn't feel any pain?" she asked.

"No," said the doctor, "She didn't wake up at all after that last stroke"

Diana clutched her ma's hand. She felt a mixture of relief and despair. Richard had his arm around her but she felt very numb and could hardly feel his touch at all.

"Is there anything else you'd like to ask me?" the doctor said.

"No" said Richard, when it became apparent that Diana wasn't going to say anything, "Thank you"

The doctor left them, telling them to take all the time they needed. But Diana really didn't want to stay much longer.

"I don't want to remember her like this" she said. "Let's just get the paperwork done and get out of here. There's so much to plan, we've got to tell people, we've got to plan the funeral, we've got to…"

"Di!" Richard said, as gently as he could, "It's ok, don't worry. We'll sort it out together. Now let's get her stuff and get the immediate things done now. We can do the rest in the morning. It's getting a bit late now, Pat will be fast asleep on the sofa by the time we get back"

Richard got out ma's bag and put the few things she had brought with her to hospital inside. He emptied out the bedside cabinet too. He hardly noticed what he was packing. He definitely didn't notice the letter addressed to Emma that was sticking out of the Carrie's War book he packed.

It was Hail who rolled himself out from under Cloud's body.

Meg bent down over Cloud, she looked up and struggled to her feet. Emma tried not to look but she couldn't help seeing a dark red stain spreading quickly over Cloud's stomach.

"Look what you did!" she screamed at Hail, pointing her gun at him.

"No!" shouted Lucy, but it was too late, Meg had already pulled the trigger and Hail, dropped his gun and clutched his arm as he fell backwards onto one of the seats.

"What did you have to do that for?" he said, agony clearly audible in his voice. "My arm!" another dark red stain was beginning to appear through his shirt.

The train was gathering momentum now, Cloud's body was rocking from side to side on the floor, and Emma and Lucy were finding it more difficult to stand up. Lucy looked pale and the red lips, that had been so carefully painted on, made her look even paler. The swaying continued as Hail continued to swear in German under his breath.

"You might as well sit down" said Meg to Emma and Lucy, "We're not going anywhere until we get to Portsmouth."

Emma and Lucy sat down on the opposite side to Hail. Was it all over? Had they won? Meg didn't look very victorious. She held her gun down by her side for a minute and was looking on the floor for the one Hail had dropped when she shot him.

She couldn't find it so she got down on all fours to look under the seat.

"Looking for this?" she heard Hail sneer as she froze. Emma wished she was braver, she could've easily jumped on top of Hail and tried to grab the gun, but she found herself stuck to her seat, the fear grabbing her and making her unable to move.

"Get off your knees, Meg" said Hail. "And give me your gun while you're at it" Meg looked across at Cloud's body, lying close by. She raised her hands, gun still in her right hand, and rose steadily to her feet. How could she have been so stupid? Turning her back on the enemy, even for a second, even when the enemy was injured, who did that? She still had her gun though, there still might be a way out of this.

She was almost up.

"Get down!" shouted Hail suddenly. The sound of machine gun fire filled the compartment.

"Get down, get down" Meg repeated, aiming her words at Emma and Lucy, who, inexplicably, hadn't moved at all. They looked at each other and suddenly Emma knew what she had to do.

She stood up quickly and brought her foot down hard onto Hail's wrist. He let go of his gun immediately and yelled out in pain. Emma grabbed the gun and pointed it shakily straight at him. Lucy had gone over to Meg and was trying to drag her to her feet and away from Hail.

"Lucy, get down, the guns! Can't you hear them?!" Meg struggled out of Lucy's grip.

"It's ok," said Lucy, "Listen". The machine guns had stopped. In their place was some sort of guitar music and a rocking drum beat.

"What?" said Meg, looking confused, "What *is* that?"

"I think the track is called 'Guns can kill'" Emma said, "Nice choice of ring tone, Lucy"

Lucy reached into the bag that Meg had given to her and pulled out her mobile phone. The music filled the carriage before abruptly stopping, "It's gone to voicemail" said Lucy with a smile.

"Your phone?" said Meg. She remembered Emma's from the night in the park. "What dreadful music you both listen to" she brushed down her skirt and checked her hair, "thank goodness!"

Lucy looked at her phone again, "It's my mum" she said with a puzzled look, "She must be wondering where I am" she looked back at Emma, "make's a change" she added quietly.

Hail was looking dazed from his position on the floor. Emma was still pointing his own gun at him and his arm was still bleeding quite heavily. "You'd better give me that" said Meg, taking over. Emma was relieved. The adrenaline was wearing off now and she felt kind of sick. The feeling got worse as she noticed Cloud's body again, still rocking to the rhythm of the train.

"You'd better sit down" said Meg, looking worried, you look like you might faint." Emma sat down heavily, Lucy slid over to her. She put her hand on her arm. "You did brilliantly!" she said.

"Well, so did you" said Emma, a little shakily,

"And so did your mum" said Meg, turning to Lucy with a little giggle. Emma recognised the giggle immediately. She was just about to say something when she felt a wave of nausea.

"I think I'm going to be sick" she said, clamping her hand over her mouth.

"Lucy, take her to the toilet" said Meg, "it's just out there on the left"

Lucy and Emma hurried out of the compartment. Emma looked back as they got into the corridor, "sorry" she said, "back in a minute"

"Don't be silly" said Meg, "I couldn't have done it without you" she looked down at Hail He was looking defeated and was staring at Cloud. He looked like he might be regretting shooting his former colleague and friend. "I'll sort out his arm, see you in a minute" Meg smiled. She gave Emma and Lucy a little wave, Emma saw a flash of silver on her wrist, then she knew.

Emma smiled too but felt her stomach lurch again. Lucy led her to the toilet. Almost inevitably when they opened the door they found themselves back in Emma's house. The train would have to carry on to Portsmouth without them.

Chapter Twenty

"Mum?" said Emma once they'd arrived back. Lucy looked out of Emma's door into the corridor.

"I can't see anyone" she said. "I'd better go". She crept towards the stairs, Emma following closely behind. She'd had an amazing night but she was glad to be home. She didn't' feel sick anymore either. As they passed the open door to the lounge, Emma noticed Pat asleep on the sofa. She wondered where her parents were but concentrated on sneaking Lucy out first. It wasn't that late but Lucy had only meant to pop in for a minute, and now it was nearly 9.30.

Emma reached for the front door. "Thanks for tonight" she said. Then she puffed out her cheeks, "That sounded so lame!"

Lucy laughed, "No, just a bit of an understatement!" she said. They both looked down at the floor.

"We can't tell anyone about this" Emma said. "No one would believe us anyway"

"Who would I tell?" said Lucy, "Everyone at school hates me and my mum barely registers my presence at all!" She gave a weak smile, Emma didn't really know what to say,

"I like you" she said quietly, Lucy's smile got wider, "and your mum did ring you tonight, remember?"

"True" said Lucy, "Maybe things are looking up!" She shrugged, "I hope Meg got Hail to Portsmouth alright"

"I'm sure she did" said Emma, she had a feeling that Meg wouldn't be visiting anymore, now the adventure was over. "She'll let us know"

"Anyway," said Lucy, "Best be getting back," she walked out into the street-lamped darkness, "see you tomorrow!"

"Bye" said Emma, closing the door behind her. She was shattered. No time to wonder about where her mum and dad were now, her bed was calling her, despite her brain still whirring with the night's events, everything would have to wait until tomorrow.

The next day the sun woke Emma up before her alarm did. It was so quiet in the house it took her a while to work out where she was, but as her mind cleared she snapped awake and sat up in bed. Meg? Had she managed to keep Hail under control all the way to Portsmouth? How had she coped travelling in the same compartment as Cloud's body? Emma desperately wanted to find out what had happened after she had left the train. But she also wanted to see Lucy and make sure she was alright too.

Emma quickly got dressed and went downstairs to see if anyone else was up. She found her mum, dad and brother all sitting solemnly round the breakfast table. Emma's heart sank, she knew what had happened.

"Nan?" she said, in a quiet voice.

Diana nodded, "It's OK, Em" she said "She just didn't wake up"

Emma felt her heart beat quicker and her eyes filled with tears. All the excitement of the past few days melted into sorrow for her Nan. She so wanted to tell her what had happened, she had wanted Nan to explain a few things too. And now? Nothing. Nothing would be answered, nothing would be explained.

"Sit down, love" said her dad. She slumped down into the chair and looked at her mum and dad. They looked tired and sad. No one said anything for a few minutes, they just thought about what life would be like now with a valuable member of the family missing.

"She was very old" Owen said at last. Diana smiled.

"She was" she said, "and if I know ma she would hate to see us sitting around here moping, let's go out and have breakfast, I really need to go somewhere"

"What about school?" Emma said, she still really wanted to see Lucy, but she wanted to be with her family as well.

"I'll give them a call" said her dad, "say you're running late, family issues"

The café was only down the road but Diana had been right, it was nice to get out the house, and everyone felt a lot better. The conversation was all about Nan, of course, but it wasn't maudlin any more, it was full of happy memories of a life lived to the full.

"I remember when I was a little girl" Diana was saying "every Saturday we used to go to old Mr Taylor's sweet shop and get a quarter of pear-drops, and, if I was very lucky, we'd take them to the cinema for a children's matinee and suck them all through the film, ma loved her sweets"

"And she loved her films too" said Richard, "she still went to the cinema nearly every week up until she had her first stroke"

Emma smiled, she remembered her Nan watching films with her too, all the Disney ones when she was younger and all the Harry Potter ones when she got old enough not to be scared. Emma was still thinking about Voldemort and Hermione when her dad broke into her thoughts.

"Oh I almost forgot" he said, "I wasn't sure when to give you this but now seems as good a time as ever." He handed Emma an envelope with her name on it, "I found it in your school reading book, the one you left at the hospital. It's from Nan."

Emma took the envelope and stared at it. Her name was written in her Nan's shaky handwriting. She tucked it into her bag, she wanted to read it on her own, with no one watching. She felt the excitement bubble in her tummy again. Maybe she would get some answers after all.

It was time to leave, they'd eaten huge doorstop bacon sandwiches and Diana said she had loads to sort out. She put her arm round Emma as they left and gave her a kiss to send her off to school with "Have a good day, Em" she said, "try not to be too sad. Talk to Lucy, she seems like a good friend who will listen".

Emma thought that was true too, and gave her mum a big hug. Richard and Owen said their goodbyes and walked off towards Owen's school near the station. Emma hurried off in the other direction. She desperately wanted to be on her own so she could read the letter.

Just before she rounded the corner to school she found a bench to sit on and she fumbled in her bag for Nan's letter. Her hands were shaking as she looked at her name again. She turned the envelope over and carefully slid her finger along the edge to open it. There was a folded piece of paper inside. Emma carefully slid it out and unfolded it.

Her heart ached a bit as she saw the familiar handwriting but the first line of the letter nearly made her heart stop altogether.

My Dear Emma,

Thank you so much for all your help. Thanks to you and Lucy, Operation Neptune went ahead as planned, (well, a day late because of the weather) and it really was the beginning of the end of the war.

Now, I know you probably worked out ages ago that I am Meg. Since the Fifties everyone has used my proper name, Margaret, but I was always Meg during the War. But let me tell you, I didn't know who this strange school girl was who helped me so much until you started to grow up and look just like her! Then I knew, I knew it was you! Please forgive me for not saying anything, I didn't want to muck up the whole of history! I was just so pleased it was you!

Neither of us will ever know how it happened but it must be something to do with some sort of tear appearing in time at just the right moment, or the special bond that binds families together, across generations and time itself. I've no idea really, have I? But whatever it was I'm so glad I got to have this adventure with you, my darling Emma.

Please don't be too sad I've gone, I haven't really. Who knows? We might even meet again one day. Have you still got my bracelet, I wonder? The one I said would always protect you. Well, I hope so, I was wearing it that night on the train and it definitely helped me. What a night that was! When you and Lucy disappeared I was kind of expecting it, but it didn't make it any easier. Hail was moaning the whole way to Portsmouth – I managed to use my tights to stop him bleeding to death, but he was such a whiner!

And poor Cloud, rest his soul, I put a coat over him but I could obviously still see him for the whole journey. I was sad about him, even though he was always so arrogant and annoying!

When we arrived at Portsmouth, Rain had already got a message ahead and we were met off the train. Hail was arrested and put in the prison van where Snow was already waiting for him. Rain and I got a pat on the back and that was that really. No medals, no ceremonies, no thanks from the King. Our work was so secret we just had to forget about it and get on with things.

I really couldn't have done it without you, all your help with the codes, the chats we had working things out, and, of course, your 21st century technology. Who'd have thought that modern music and mobile phones would save the day?

So, thank you Emma, my beautiful, clever great granddaughter, I love you and I will always be with you. And as I said before, who knows? We might even meet again?

Just keep your eyes open,

All my love

Nan

Emma read it all again and blinked back the tears that were filling her eyes and spilling down her cheeks. She had known that Meg felt familiar all through this, but she didn't really know for sure that it was Nan until she'd heard that giggle last night, and seen the silver flash of bracelet, the pieces had fallen into place. What a wonderful adventure to share with one of her favourite people in the world!

She laughed out loud when she read the bit about Hail again. "What's so funny?" said a voice behind her. It was Lucy.

Emma wiped her eyes and gave her a watery smile, "Why aren't you at school?"

Lucy sat down next to Emma, "I'm late" she said, "No big deal"

Emma looked at her, she thought that she looked a bit different, "Well, I know why I'm late" Emma said, "But why are you?"

"My mum" said Lucy, "She wanted to talk and she kind of wouldn't stop!" Lucy looked happy.

Emma didn't really know much about Lucy's home life but she knew that Lucy and her mum didn't appear to get on at all, so it *was* a big deal that they were talking. Emma left it at that, she was glad that Lucy seemed happy but she desperately wanted to tell her all about her Nan and the letter and the end of this whole saga.

"I couldn't sleep last night, how do you think Meg got on after we left?" Lucy said.

"Well…" said Emma, and handed Lucy the letter.

To be continued…?

Key words and terms

Operation Neptune – The codename for the Normandy landings, (the Allied (Britain and her Allies) invasion of France- the attempt to free France from Nazi occupation.

Operation Overlord – The codename for the overall Battle of Normandy which began with Operation Neptune.

Operation Fortitude – The British deception plan for the Germans. It led the Germans to believe that the main target for the Normandy landings was the Pas de Calais- much further east than the real plan.

D-Day Landings – Another name for the Allied invasion of Normandy.

Normandy – area of Northern France

Abwehr – The German military intelligence organisation – their spy agency.

MI5 – The British Intelligence organisation – The British secret service – the British spy agency.

Bletchley – During the war the German secret codes were broken here.

The Blitz – was a period of constant bombing of British cities by the Nazis.

Air Raid – an attack by enemy planes dropping bombs.

Luftwaffe – Gernan airforce

Alison lives in North London with her husband and two children. She enjoys writing stories and poems, and is also a keen runner. She is a History teacher at a local comprehensive school. "Friendship and Spies" is her first book.